Split Pea Soup

A Ghost Story

Split Pea Soup

A Ghost Story

by

Victor Cooper

LitPrime Solutions
21250 Hawthorne Blvd
Suite 500, Torrance, CA 90503
www.litprime.com
Phone: 1-800-981-9893

Published by LitPrime Solutions   01/04/2024

ISBN: 979-8-88703-333-4(sc)
ISBN: 979-8-88703-334-1(e)

Library of Congress Control Number: 2023924588

For my spooky girls, Nicole and Gabrielle

Contents

Chapter 1

Norman sat in the shadows near the corner of his room touching and taking inventory of the deep cuts on his face. He found himself gazing across the room as he was coming out of another mindless daze. He wasn't staring at anything in particular, but as he slowly gained awareness, he realized he was looking across his empty room at the metal bed. Lacking a mattress or covers, there was only a cold rectangular frame with a mesh of wires supported by springs. He stared without interest.

The gash over Norman's left brow and the cut under his right eye still felt fresh. Though not bleeding, the wounds were moist and opened to reveal the tissue separating his skin from his skull. He thoughtlessly touched his thin lips as he continued to stare across the room.

Sitting against the wall on the floor with his knees bent upward, Norman was barefoot. He always wore the same clothes, a set of black trousers held up by a tightly cinched black belt and a button-up light blue Sunday shirt with the left collar bent up against his pencil-thin neck. His clothes hung loosely off his scrawny eight-year-old frame.

Norman moved aside his stringy black bangs to once again touch one of his open wounds. This time he pinched it using his thumb and middle finger in the hope it would stay closed for good. It was a gesture of hope that he wouldn't always awaken to be reminded of the pain and torture he had endured.

The corner of his room was his usual spot to sit and stare. He frequently would find himself coming around while sitting in this shadowy part of the room. Sometimes when he began to focus his vision, he would realize he was not in his room but in the basement or in Mrs. Crawford's room. He's even found himself on the roof looking down over the edge. But this doesn't startle or worry Norman. On occasion he may get up and return to his room but usually he would sit and stare at nothing until he would fall away into his idleness until sooner or later, he came around to having awareness again, back in his room sitting in the corner. To say Norman slept during these outages is not correct. If he slept, he would dream. And Norman never dreamed. To him, he simply would come and go; light fades on, light fades off.

The silvery foil covering the window to the left of Norman's head was beginning to peel away from the lower right corner revealing a speckled beam of light targeting the floor near Norman's foot. He slowly moved his left hand outward to meet the light. The mild reflection off his palm irritated his eyes. He held his hand steady and then rotated it until the dim light shone upon the back of his fingers. Like the cuts on his face, his left hand was a reminder of his suffering. His hand was grotesquely flattened with purple blotches and was at least an inch longer than his other hand. Holding both hands in the glow of the outside light, he could see the contrast of the bruised coloring on his damaged hand compared to his usual pale, greenish-gray skin. With his normal hand Norman touched the cuts on his face.

The room was silent. In fact, the whole building was completely quiet. Usually even the slightest movement or whispers from any of the others in the building could be detected. Although Norman preferred to be by himself, he kept his door to the hallway slightly open.

His room was positioned in the corner of the building and had two tall, narrow windows. The one near the bed frame was boarded up with plywood from the outside. The window nearest him was covered from the inside with tin foil and black electrical tape. This suited Norman just fine as he had no interest in what was outside.

A bare bulb hanging from the hallway ceiling provided a strip of light against his wall contrasted by the sharp, angular shadow created from the opened door. Other than the bed frame, there was only an empty bookshelf occupying the aging wood floor. The dark, cinder block walls were void of anything decorative interrupted only by a broken mirror hanging above a sink.

Norman was again transfixed in a stare. Instead of the bare, metal bed frame, he was gazing at his hand as he moved it back and forth through the mottled beam of light. Back and forth, back and forth he slowly waved his long floppy hand. As his focus began to blur and his attention receded, it occurred to him that the rhythm of the light reflecting off his hand was like the pendulum of a clock. A fleeting thought as he slowly disappeared into his next void. A pointless notion as there was no need for a clock in Norman's world. His existence was simply made up of brief periods of awareness. How long were these periods of darkness and light? It didn't matter. He was content to just stare. Stare at his bed, stare at his wall, his sink, his door. All he could do was stare because Norman had no eyelids.

Chapter 2

"**D**amn it!"

Steven wasn't angry about the detour; he was angry at himself for being an idiot. From the moment he woke up this morning he could only think about the details of that stupid party last night. How close he came to tumbling over the edge and totally losing it. His body ached. Well, half of his body. He was exhausted but he wasn't hungover. In fact, Steven's never been hungover.

Plodding along at a snail's pace in his cream-colored Land Rover, the detour was probably the distraction he needed. Instead of heading south-east to the business park, he would instead have to take a slower drive up through the hills on the west side of town.

The rain came down in a thick mist adding weight to the leaves stuck to his windshield. In a long sigh he tried to recall how many years it had been since he had a full-blown meltdown, six, eight maybe? He didn't dwell on that memory. He didn't dare think about that.

The party yesterday was a neighborhood barbecue in celebration of the advent of autumn. Or it was an excuse to grill some meat and get drunk outdoors before it got too cold. Even though everyone came wearing jackets, it was pleasant and dry enough to play horseshoes and softball. There was a TV in the community recreation room to watch football which Steven preferred.

Even just three years ago Steven wouldn't have been able to come to such a social gathering because of the risk of having one of his episodes and completely losing control. It was mostly just a matter of willpower and keeping his mind focused. If he allowed himself to dwell on the possibility of having a breakdown he might easily get caught in the spiral of uncertainty and fear. And fear was the final step toward panic and an inevitable outburst. It was a self-fulfilling process. It just took that initial spark.

At the party Steven met an oriental woman, probably in her early 30's, named Kim. He'd never seen her before but recognized her boyfriend from his building, an overweight ex-marine with the obligatory anchor tattoo on his forearm.

Steven caught her looking at him on a few occasions. Could she be attracted to me, he thought?

Steven wasn't hideous but he knew better than to think a woman could spontaneously be interested in him. Even though there were no visible scars from the accident, the left side of his face had a slight paralysis causing a bit of laziness around his eye and a crooked mouth. He stood five feet ten inches and had dark brown hair, long enough to tuck behind his ears. His weak jaw correctly depicted his meek and timid disposition.

He nonchalantly watched Kim at a table with five other women. One after the other she read each of the women's palms and told them their fortune. There was a lot of laughter but occasionally there was a gasp of awe. Before long Kim was flitting about the room reading everyone's palm. Steven cynically wondered if her line of business was to provide cheap entertainment at unnecessary parties.

Steven was pouring himself a beer, which he had no intention of drinking, when he noticed Kim approaching with an empty plastic cup. As he reached the tap over her tilted cup he asked, "Is it my turn yet to hear my future?"

"It isn't real. I'm just pretending." Kim said looking down at her beer.

"If you don't really tell fortunes you're very good at acting like you do. How long have you been doing this?"

Kim looked up and into Steven's eyes and gave him a half smile. She paused for a moment, bit her lower lip and then walked away.

Well, that answered my question, he thought. She's not attracted to me but probably just considers me interesting, interesting like a carnival freak.

Predictably, Steven let this small awkward moment get to him. Being hypersensitive, he felt his heart rate pick up. His palms were damp and his left eye twitched.

His automatic defense mechanism he had worked so diligently to achieve kicked in. He immediately saturated his mind with pointless mental challenges to prevent any possibility of becoming overly emotional. This time he reacted by forcing himself to work through a simple algebraic equation. Sometimes he would occupy his mind with other math problems such as trigonometry calculations, square root of large numbers, whatever it took to create a mental distraction. Steven has gone through these formulas in his head a thousand times. All he needed to do was whip up some new numbers to plug into the process.

These mental exercises required his full attention. As long as he stayed focused, continued turning the inner gears of his intellect, he would pacify that part of his brain he wished would stay dormant, at least long enough to be off alone where there was no pressure to compute his brain into exhaustion. But if he couldn't suppress it, it would be out there for all to see, to see Steven literally tear himself to shreds from the inside out. But Steven was confident. This was a very minor setback compared to the episodes he experienced almost every day at work. He can relax and move on and at least pretend he is a normal person at this stupid party.

Later on, after the football game on TV had ended, the sun began to set in the west as light gray clouds above yielded a slight drizzle. He had spent enough time at the party to give himself credit for being social and now it was time to go home. Before he could leave, Steven was a little startled to look up and see Kim standing square in front of him about eight feet away blocking the way to the door. "Do this," she said, holding up her left hand with her fingers pointing straight up and her thumb at a ninety-degree angle to the side. It was obvious she wanted him to mirror her left hand with his right, revealing his palm albeit at a slight distance. Upon seeing Steven's raised hand, Kim's eyes grew wide, and her jaw relaxed. Her hand slowly fell to her side as she shifted her eyes away from Steven. As she turned her head to the side and toward the floor, once again, she just walked away. Her bonehead ex-marine boyfriend chuckled and shook his head.

At first Steven chuckled a little as well and thought how odd it would be that Kim would single him out like this. Looking at his right palm he didn't see anything strange, no unusual lines or marks shaped like three sixes.

Then without the slightest warning, not even a hint of an impending tantrum, he felt his left hand stiffen. He looked away from his right palm to his contorting hand and felt the sudden rush of terror fill his face. His left hand jerked outward and then slammed back into his chest, grabbing and twisting his shirt. Steven didn't have a chance to think through any kind of math or physics problems or even tic-tac-toe, he had to get away immediately. He felt his left leg stiffening as he attempted large strides toward the door. He desperately grabbed his left wrist trying to control himself before he could rip his own shirt off. Without warning, his left hand lunged at his throat and started to choke him. It was all he could do to wrestle with his hand until he dislodged it from its grasp. He ran out of the recreation room as fast as he could.

By the time he had half-jogged the two blocks back to his apartment, he was sweating heavily and gasping for breath. His panic had subsided but now he became aware of the physical pain he felt on the entire left side of his body. Trying to put the key in his front door occupied his mind just enough to sense he was starting to calm down. Within a few seconds of being inside he was able to manage a glass of water. He grabbed a pencil and rapidly began putting letters in the blank boxes of a New York Times crossword puzzle. Steven took a breath and then ramped up his focus on the puzzle until he was in control again. He took a deep breath and only hoped he hadn't made too much of a scene, running away from the party.

"Hey, pick it up!" The construction site sign-holder was yelling through Steven's closed window only about two inches away. Steven put the Land Rover in first gear and sped towards the traffic which had distanced itself a few hundred feet ahead.

He wondered how he would manage at work today. He would need to ignore what happened at the party and be always prepared and in all circumstances to take charge of his mental focus. "Be the laser beam" he said out loud to himself. He checked his shirt pocket to ensure he had a pad and pen at the ready in case there was a need for expressing pi or working through the Lorentz formula of time dilation.

Driving over the crest of the first hill in the western neighborhood, he caught a glimpse of the old Catholic church about a quarter of a mile away. It had been years since Steven was in this part of town. He spent his early childhood out here somewhere although he didn't remember even a minute of it. Instead of following the long line of cars through the designated detour route, he decided to break to the right and visit this strange eclectic old suburb.

Every few blocks the landscape of homes and businesses changed its face. Heading west, as the elevation slowly climbed, there were Victorian style houses most of which had recently gone through some kind of refurbishing effort. Some had added features such as turrets and bay windows for the classic look while others took on a yuppie color scheme of bright walls with contrasting borders, highlighting the windows, doors and eaves. Beyond this neighborhood the trees were taller and denser consisting of cottonwoods, ash and maples. Properties appeared larger because the houses were smaller and less obtrusive than the Victorians. Most of these houses were A-frame ranch style with either brick walls or wood siding.

Separating these two neighborhoods was the Catholic church oddly juxtaposed alongside an old pub with a hanging sign that simply said "Tavern."

Steven slowed the car. From this point of view, he could see across the hillside a further mix of dilapidated houses as well as more recently built mansions spotting the ridge spanning the south-western edge of town. He knew he spent many years in one of these houses, but he didn't have any idea which one it was.

He stopped scanning the area once he recognized the beige brick walls and green roof of the mental hospital. Maybe taking this drive wasn't such a good idea, he thought to himself. Steven had never been inside the hospital, but he was uneasily aware of its existence. During his teenage years when he was questioning everything about his life, his grandmother would reassure him that his mother did not suffer while she lived there during her final days.

"It was a well-deserved time of rest," Grandma would say.

Steven didn't need to confront thoughts about his mother today. He couldn't recall ever being with her but the idea of placing himself in a time when they were together could be just enough to spark an unwanted reaction, especially in his shaky mental state following last night's attack.

Turning right to avoid the sight of the mental facility, Steven now headed north in the opposite direction of his office building. He wasn't pressed for time. He usually arrived at work earlier than everyone else so he could get into the mindset of playing the professionally dressed geek at a big dork factory. But he then thought better of wasting his time and began to backtrack to the detour route.

Before making another right turn to head east, Steven was intrigued by an unusual black building off to his left in the recess between two hills. It was mostly obscured by tall cottonwood trees though he could see that the building took on an almost perfect cube shape. Instead of turning right, he went toward the building to get a closer look.

Steven stopped short of the long dirt driveway that extended about fifty or sixty feet from the building. He could see round river stones exposed in spots on the drive where tire ruts cleared the dirt. The grounds were covered with fresh golden leaves except for gaps that revealed packed down, older brown leaves that were never raked. The perimeter of the property was not obvious as the dense trees hid any sign of civilization and the rising landscape behind the building led to the forest.

Steven turned off the Land Rover motor and rolled down his window and listened. It was unnaturally quiet except for the faint sound of static as the drizzling rain impacted the crisp leaves.

The building had a menacing if not an offensive look about it. It was an aberration to the scenic surroundings. It stood three stories high and was entirely black. Not deep glossy or ebony black, more like a dirty charcoal black. Maybe on a sunny day the light would give the effect of it being a dark, dusty shade of gray. On the roof, toward the south side, Steven noticed a vent pipe with a conical top. It was about seven feet long, crooked, leaning toward the rear of the building. It occurred to him the reason this pipe stood out was because it was the only asymmetrical characteristic of the entire structure. On the front side the top two floors each had four high, rectangular windows. Some were boarded up and painted black. Steven could see torn shades and ragged curtains from within the other windows. The first floor only had two windows separated by a front entrance. The door was large and appeared heavy and, of course, was painted black. A small wooden porch in front of the entrance had just enough room next to the door for a chair and a shovel leaning against the wall.

This was an odd building in an odd part of town. Steven looked at the simple pattern of the textured molding that separated the walls from the roof, which appeared to extend around the entire rim of the building. There didn't seem to be any rain gutters. There also was no sign of the inhabitants. Steven looked for either a mailbox or address numbers but didn't see them attached to the building nor out by the road.

It wasn't the blunt starkness of this structure that bothered Steven; it was the grim cell-block appearance of the cinder block walls. Each rectangle was perfectly placed resulting in smoothly textured walls and sharp, precisely edged corners. He couldn't help but numbly stare at the building. One could almost fall for the illusion that the cube was inverted, creating a dark corner in the landscape.

The streaking gray sky felt cold and heavy. Steven rolled up his window and put his car into reverse.

Chapter 3

Thirty years earlier when Steven was nine, his fourth-grade class took a field trip to a farm twenty miles outside of town. It was the first field trip of the year and, literally, Mrs. Ortega's students spent the morning in a field. The ten-acre corn maze was shaped like a giant Triceratops dinosaur. The corn stalks stood at least five feet high and were planted in rows dense enough to create walls too thick to see through.

Each student was paired up with a buddy and provided with one map and one whistle. In case any of the students panicked or were still trying to find their way out by the time the lunch bell rang, they were instructed to stay put and blow their whistle just once a minute until help arrived. Steven's partner was Toby, a plump freckle-faced redhead boy with a flattop haircut. Toby insisted on carrying the whistle around his neck while Steven held onto the map.

It seemed pointless to Steven that someone would take the painstaking effort to make such a big dinosaur design in the corn field. Other than seeing the image on the map, who would really know what it was? Crop dusters? A spy satellite? Maybe this field is all just a bunch of lines plowed out one afternoon by a drunken old farmer. Or maybe it was intended to be something entirely different, like a pig or a helicopter, but by the time it was finished it looked more like a Triceratops.

The entrance and the exit of the maze were near each other separated by an old windmill nestled in a thicket of corn shoots. The metal windmill was about twenty-five feet high yielding a small mewing sound as the slight fall breeze turned the crooked metal blades at the top. Steven tried to keep his eyes fixed on the windmill as he and Toby were backtracking out of the first dead-end, they encountered in the maze. If he could keep it in sight, they could use the windmill to help guide them to the exit. However, it wasn't long before it was completely hidden by the tall rows of corn.

Mrs. Ortega had instructed the kids to pay attention to the map and keep it facing north as the "N" and the arrow at the top of the sheet indicated. Since the sun was still rising in the east, the light should be shining from the right making it easy to keep the map correctly oriented to the north. Not one child understood what she was talking about.

Steven and Toby found themselves reaching the windmill only about 45 minutes into the excursion. They figured they must be the first ones out since they were told it should take at least two hours. Somehow, they must have stumbled onto a secret passage or maybe this was the entrance again. Toby gleefully pranced across the threshold out of the maze to the open dirt clearing; you'd think it was his first day out of prison. But Steven was reluctant to leave the corn field just yet. He decided to hide in the cluster of corn stalks by the windmill and sit by himself until they rang the bell for lunch. Steven worked his way between the stalks without damaging them and sat down at the bottom of the windmill's steel structure. He felt the comfort of isolation being away from everyone else, especially that dweeb Toby.

Steven was a loner. He hung out and played with other boys occasionally but for the most part he would rather be off by himself. His grandmother always praised him for his independence and self-reliance. Steven would learn years later that she would say just about anything to help give him a sense of esteem. Even if Steven was different from everyone else, there was no reason he should turn out to be anything less than an intelligent and respected human being. But sometimes Grandma's positive spin on everything was beyond ridiculous. Back in first grade when Steven barfed at his desk, she said how lucky he was to purge all that bad stuff inside that was keeping him from learning his ABC's. She had convinced Steven he was going to be the smartest kid in his class because he blew chunks of stupidity all over the classroom floor.

It didn't seem like very much time had passed before the farmer began ringing the bell. He enthusiastically banged on the inner sides of the hanging triangle like he'd been waiting for this moment all morning. Steven could hear the kids playing outside of the maze and heard only a few whistles from within. After a few minutes he overheard Mrs. Ortega yelling at Toby for leaving his partner behind in the maze.

"The buddy system only works if you stay with your buddy at ALL TIMES!" she hollered.

Steven looked up at the windmill and watched as the slow-moving clouds gave the illusion the tower was moving. The windmill seemed tall and imposing from this angle. Considering what it would take to climb all the way to the top gave Steven a slight adrenaline rush. The thought of scaling the mill was a little scary yet it was irresistible. Even if it was rusty and dirty, it would be the perfect way to see if this maze really looked like a Triceratops.

"Steven! Come on, let's go," Mrs. Ortega was calling.

This will be great, Steven thought. From the windmill I'll be able to watch them search for me in the maze.

So he started climbing. After the first ten feet the windmill seemed a little shaky but once Steven noticed that three of the four legs were firmly mounted to the cement base below, he continued to creep upward. He noticed his hands were turning powder-orange from the rust. It was noticeably cooler up here than in the protective corn stalks. Steven was about three feet from the top when he heard the farmer yelling at him to get down. This was followed by Mrs. Ortega frantically screaming something about no lunch and sitting on the bus. Steven had his back facing the open area outside of the maze. As he held onto the crisscross steel structure tightly with his right hand, Steven leaned outward, twisting his upper body to face the gazing onlookers of the fourth-grade class. He dramatically waved at the kids and his teacher as he shouted out loud, "Ahoy-eee!"

Steven's stomach moved up into his throat the moment he felt the steel structure begin to bend. The sound of metal twisting upon itself was at first a low creaking vibration but quickly became a roar of intense screeching and gnashing. As the crumpling windmill accelerated toward the ground, Steven could only hold on and watch in what seemed like slow motion as he headed downward. Steven held his right hand tight as he saw the other kids rising upward to meet him.

Then, all at once, when the windmill was bent over at a right angle and the spinning fan blades were about twelve feet off the ground, it abruptly stopped falling. Steven was thrown swiftly to the dirt. He partially landed on his feet at first but then went down hard on his back and head. He was stunned and found himself out of breath. Disoriented, he looked up to see the kids in his class slowly take steps backward giving him room as his dizzying head swayed in a small circle.

Compared to the horribly loud sound of the clashing metal just a moment ago, it was oddly silent. Then Steven began to hear ringing in both of his ears. Dazed, he looked to the left and then to the right at all his classmates. Their eyes and their mouths were opened wide in astonishment. A few of the kids had a look of delight with raised eyebrows as laughter began to stretch back their lips. It was difficult to determine Mrs. Ortega's reaction as she was covering her mouth with both hands.

Feeling his emotions welling up inside, Steven didn't need this opportunity to cry. But he wasn't sure he even had the energy or the wind to let out a whimper. Instead of crying, he slowly rose to his feet. At first his knees shook and his head felt too big to hoist, but in a single motion Steven was standing up and feeling less likely to start bawling.

He took a few small breaths and stood motionless with his arms at his sides as he looked into the eyes of his peers. He could sense his left hand was trembling. Some of the kids looked on with pity and some with ridicule. All of them looked like cartoon characters. He could hear nothing except the ringing in his ears. Then he noticed that everyone's gaze had slowly shifted upward. Steven followed their eyes toward the sky until his head was bent backwards looking straight above him. The clotted metal of the windmill had broken free, and all Steven could see were the blades of the wheel rushing down, falling directly toward his face. It was all Steven could do to try and lunge forward out of the path of the sharp blades, but it was too late. As he ducked his head down and began to bend his knees in a forward motion, his reaction was halted when one of the windmill blades struck the top of his head breaking through his skull, slicing deep into his brain.

Steven's head was horrifically dissected by the fallen windmill, but he was able to continue standing. He was only slightly aware of what was happening. He didn't feel any pain but knew he had been hit hard in the head. He was in a stupor, peering out from within a thick bubble. Instead of collapsing to the ground as the weight of the windmill sticking out of his cranium should dictate, Steven mindlessly attempted to take a step forward in a sick, wobbly effort. But he was powerless to move freely, being held back by the mass of metal.

Mrs. Ortega screamed in horror as she struggled with her tightly clenched fists pressed against the sides of her face. The old farmer, wide-eyed and slack jawed, rushed toward Steven but froze once he came within five feet. He held out his hands in a gesture of help but was reluctant to touch the impaled boy.

Steven remained on his feet with his arms spread outward as though he was trying to balance himself. His right eye had rolled back into his head and his left eye stared blankly towards the ground. Blood was streaming down the middle of his forehead between his eyes, curving past his nose and mouth, dripping down off the center of his chin.

For a few more seconds Steven's body remained standing but began to tremble and shake from his head and neck down through his waist, hips and knees. Finally, his body became completely limp and crumpled down to the ground where he landed square on his butt.

The blade of the windmill still firmly embedded in the top of Steven's head kept him from falling completely to the ground. Instead, he sat hunched forward with his chin buried in his chest.

Steven intently closed his eyes. He listened to the ringing in his ears until he finally drifted into blissful unconsciousness.

After that unfortunate October day, the old slack jawed farmer closed his corn field to the public for good. And all the boys and girls of Mrs. Ortega's fourth grade class, who had gazed at the twisted windmill protruding from Steven's head, would remember this horror show for the rest of their lives. Some more than others.

Chapter 4

The low, guttural creaking sound from the meat grinder could be heard echoing down the hallway and throughout the building. Slow deliberate rotations of the metal handle groaned in agony from years of wear. Norman held his elbows as he leaned against the door jamb of his room. He found himself staring down into the shadows of the far end of the second-floor hall where an empty light socket hung from the ceiling. Mrs Crawford's room was down there. Her door was shut but because her meat grinder was bolted onto a counter, the creaking and groaning could be heard and felt through the walls and floor. Sometimes Norman could hear the grinding from the basement where the drainpipes from each room converged to a common sewage outlet. He could hear practically any noise from any room as the sound waves seemed to just crawl through pipes.

Norman was fading in and fading out and only had a partial awareness of his vacant gaze down the narrow hall. He mindlessly touched the cuts on his face as the sound of the meat grinder oozed into his consciousness. Without giving it any thought, he found himself slowly walking in the direction of Mrs Crawford's room, holding his elbows and sinking his head down into his shoulders. The old wooden floor responded to Norman's slight steps with tiny squeaks.

The end of the hall was completely dark except for a bar of light extending out from the gap below Mrs. Crawford's door. Norman carefully crept along the hallway with his right shoulder lightly dragging against the wall until he eventually arrived at the dead end. Looking down at the light stretching across the floor to the other side of the hall, the glare caused Norman to shield his eyes with his long, mangled hand. Norman stood for a moment, occasionally looking between his fingers at the bright light allowing his eyes to adjust. Eventually he dropped his hand back to his elbow briefly touching his lips along the way.

Norman stared at the doorknob.

The grinding within was steady and continuous.

The door suddenly opened on its own with a barely audible click. The white vertical line of light from floor to ceiling was initially an inch thick but rapidly widened until the end of the hall was completely overtaken with light, extending a long shadow of Norman's little body down the hallway. Norman covered his eyes again and this time he kept them covered long enough to count twenty turns of the meat grinder.

As he slowly moved his hand outward to control the exposure of light to his unprotected eyes. He noticed the familiar feeling of being light on his feet. And then he felt himself begin to fade, to slowly disappear again into another void. Usually, he would just let himself go, there was rarely a reason to stay focused and fight the natural feeling of submission. But this time Norman chose to be alert. He wanted to see Mrs. Crawford and what she was grinding. So, he quickly dropped his hand forcing the shock of the light to snap him out of his waning awareness. He winced and stepped back as the light stunned him.

Norman heard the woman from upstairs. It was hard to hear her at first as she made a sort of hissing sound followed by gasping, apparently having trouble taking a breath. The hissing quieted a little with a second effort although it was accompanied by a low rasp. There was a third attempt but this time the hissing was overtaken by a trembling cry of frustration. Norman could hear her struggle to suck in a few deep breaths before she began to sob.

The grinding had abruptly stopped. Norman, while listening to the crying from upstairs, had become unaware that he was staring directly into the bright light emitting from inside the room. Mrs. Crawford made a noise, a hoarse choking sound. Norman couldn't tell if she was gagging or attempting to laugh. He patiently allowed his vision to come to him as he began to make out the shape of Mrs. Crawford sitting on her stool bathed in white light. His eyes hurt but through the light he could make out the old woman's cat-eyed, black sunglasses she always wore. The rest of Mrs. Crawford's image was hard to distinguish as her pale, taunt skin and wiry hair faded into the light emanating from the uncovered window from behind her.

Norman watched Mrs. Crawford. The longer he stared, the details of her frail old body became more apparent. She was hunched forward with both of her hands fixed to the handle attached to the unusually long arm of the meat grinder. She wore an oversized white apron over her gray dress as her legs dangled from the height of the stool.

The woman from upstairs was quiet for a few moments. But at last, she was able to gain enough strength to blurt out something, "Steeeee-ven." It was rare to hear anything other than moaning and crying from that recluse. She was usually too weak or too delusional to form actual words. Her good for nothing long and lanky body lay useless on her bed.

Norman and Mrs. Crawford remained still, and both listened with anticipation.

"Sssssssteeee-ven," the scrawny woman upstairs began to wail repeatedly, "Steee-ee-ven, Steee-ee-ven!"

Norman was delighted at the idea of the mummy head woman upstairs acting like she had a brain. He continued to be amused by her whining but thought he might have heard giggling. The sound wasn't coming from the zombie woman but instead was being made by another voice on the third floor. It was the bag lady down the hall. She wasn't really laughing but instead was mocking the woman's cries by "boo-hooing" in a sarcastic, sing-song voice.

This seemed to agitate the woman who began to shout out loud, "Steven… Steeeeeeee-ven."

The bag lady sang along in a high-pitched falsetto, "Steeeeeeee-ven… Steeeeeeee-ven."

As the two from upstairs competed, Mrs. Crawford resumed cranking the handle but now with a little more vigor. Norman was amused by the way she committed her entire upper body to the full turn of the crank. On the downward motion she would lurch forward throwing her torso toward the floor and then would erect herself upward from her waist through her shoulders, reaching high with both hands as she completed the circle. Even with her tiny body with spindly arms, she was able to leverage a considerable amount of grinding power because of the ridiculously long radius of the handle.

Mrs. Crawford was now making a cackling sound to add to the chorus from above. With her jaw forever locked in a gaping wide silent scream, she was unfortunately unable to utilize her tongue or lips to form words. Instead, she let out a formless moan broken up by chortles and coughs. Even though she was hunched forward toward the meat grinder, her head was unnaturally angled backward, and seemed to be stuck that way. With each rotation of the long arm, her gaze shifted from the ceiling to the wall and back again to the ceiling. Her backward and forward jerking motions were so exaggerated it almost appeared the grinder was controlling her. It was obvious now the Mrs Crawford was becoming hysterical with delight, hacking out spasms of "Phyllis Diller" laughter.

Norman crinkled his nose pulling at his upper lip which exposed his little teeth. He held a sinister grimace as he turned away from Mrs. Crawford's room and began to walk back down the hall to his own room, unnoticed. Instead of holding his elbows, Norman's hands were now on top of his head as he stood tall, walking on his tiptoes. There was electricity in the air of this decrepit building. He could feel it in his bones. As he walked down the hallway, he silently mouthed the syllables along with the frenetic cries from upstairs. He attempted to spin on his left foot but after a half-pivot he walked the remainder of the circle with his arms outstretched like a veering airplane. His wings were angled downward in a sharp turn toward his left side where his long floppy hand was extended.

"Steeeeeee-ven," the woman upstairs screamed as loud as she could. "Steven, come home!"

Chapter 5

Sitting in his office, Steven stared at his reflection from the glare on his computer screen. He was wearing his reading glasses which were not necessary but added credibility to his nerd persona. He knew everyone at work thought he was a weirdo, but it was much better if they thought of him as an *intellectual* weirdo. As far as everyone in his office was concerned, Steven was an accomplished, smart, quiet and quirky Systems Auditor. He rarely socialized and kept to himself in his westward facing office. He was usually seen with his face buried in his computer console.

A few minutes earlier Steven's boss stopped by making his usual rounds. Drake was a gruff, impatient fathead who thought it was necessary to have a daily tantrum in order to keep up productivity. Apparently, this was what he was paid to do.

Steven had a headache. He wasn't sure if it was from the episode yesterday still on his mind or if it was Drake. He hated Drake. Maybe his headache was due to these ridiculously bright lights recently installed in the building. Why would a firm that employs over one hundred Software Engineers, who stare at computer monitors all day, install such bright lights? Steven had amused himself with management conspiracy theories where subtle torture techniques were applied for purposes of mind control. It had recently become noticeable that workers throughout the building were getting a zombie-like pallor with dark circles under their eyes. The contrast of the bright office lights made the rainy outdoors seem unnaturally dark for ten o'clock in the morning.

Steven had a feeling of dread. It wasn't so much from his constant worrying over losing control but more the lingering lowly feeling he would get for days after having an outburst, even if it was minor like the one yesterday at the party. It was a recovery process he had dealt with for most of his life. Usually, the day after was the worst. He couldn't explain why, but more than anything he felt a sense of loss.

The windmill accident had left Steven without any memories of his childhood. He could remember only as far back as his grandmother visiting him during his long hospital stay. He remembered his struggle returning to school and how difficult it was to try and catch up with the rest of the class. He never did. Steven completed sixth grade when he was 14 years old. Even though he made considerable strides during the following three years, he never completed his junior year, dropping out of high school when he was 18 at the time his original classmates were graduating. The next four years were the most challenging for Steven. Not only was he having difficulty making a life for himself working as a clerk at a grocery store, but he struggled to deal with the daily battles with mental problems because of the accident. He was 20 years old when he completed the High School GED exam and received his diploma. He was 22 when his grandmother died leaving Steven entirely on his own. He refused the prescribed medical and mental therapy once he became an adult. This was partially his grandmother's fault. She was so protective of Steven that she didn't want to upset him by even talking about the accident or his condition. She praised every one of his micro accomplishments like when he was relearning to brush his teeth. She told him he didn't need anyone's help in accomplishing anything. Apparently, she felt ongoing doctor's visits were a reminder of his problems causing damage to his self-esteem.

It wasn't the physical consequences of the accident that turned Steven into an outcast. It only took a few years before he recovered to the point where there was hardly any evidence of his head being split open. His hair grew over the scar and his facial paralysis was subtle enough that it was barely noticeable. None the less, Steven acquired a mental condition that degraded over time causing him to be withdrawn and very self-conscience. It was almost two years after the accident when Steven first discovered his second "self". He initially kept it a secret from his grandmother because he didn't want her to think what he feared at the time, that he was under some kind of demonic possession. It all happened one day when he was getting dressed. As he finished buttoning up his shirt he was stunned as his left hand independently rebelled by unbuttoning his shirt from top to bottom. It was as though someone else had taken control of his whole left arm. As he began to button up his shirt again, his left hand slapped his right hand. This deeply disturbed Steven. But at the time he had no clue how this condition would have an impact on just about every day of his life.

Sitting in his office staring at his computer screen occasionally glancing out the window, Steven felt the onset of a familiar childhood emotion. It was as though it was his first day at school. It was that feeling of uneasiness, of being in a new situation with a new teacher and students, the smell of chalk and pencil sharpeners, and the dread of being stuck in a classroom until next summer. Steven felt like he was an insecure little boy again. He fidgeted with his computer mouse pretending like he was engaged in his work hoping the feeling would soon pass.

As unnerving and upsetting as his episodes could be, Steven was fascinated by the brief glimpses of lost childhood memories they seemed to resurrect as an after effect. Usually, it was just an odd feeling like the one he was having today but sometimes he would remember playing with a particular toy or talking with someone back in the time before the accident. It was kind of like trying to remember a dream after just waking up while the residual feeling was still present. On a few occasions he remembered his mother. Once after a major outburst, he distinctly recalled watching her gracefully dance by herself as she listened to a piano song on a scratchy record. Years later he learned that this melody was "Clare de Lune" by Debussy. Maybe he had assigned her face to his memories from old photographs. At times he could vaguely remember her soft feminine features and long blond hair. Recalling the way she moved in a solo ballet with an expression of romance and reflection, Steven didn't feel love for his mother. Instead, these brief memories of her usually caused him to feel pity. He didn't understand why but he truly felt sorry for his mother even though these visions of her were calm and beautiful.

Steven turned away from his computer and investigated the hall where he watched as some of his coworkers gathered by the coffee maker shooting the breeze. Sometimes it was puzzling why it was so necessary for people to intermingle multiple times a day. It was like they had an addiction to talking. It was apparent that Drake was spotted in the area as the group quickly dispersed.

Steven felt like a charlatan, a fake among the geeky engineers he worked with. He did more than an adequate job and by all rights earned his paycheck, but he never felt like he belonged. He didn't go to college and earn a degree. Instead, he survived purely on his wits and the knowledge he gathered along the way. He wondered if some of the others didn't just dress the part and fake their careers as well. He just knew he didn't fit in this so-called professional world. But he didn't have a clue what else he would do if he quit his job. He realized that he should probably be thankful. In fact, for such a basket case, he should be ecstatic he has a job to go to every day. With that passing thought, Steven continued to dawdle the morning hours away hoping the earlier visit from Drake was the last of the day.

Not really feeling hungry, Steven forced himself to get up and walk to the cafeteria centrally located on the first floor of the office building. As he stood in line his mind wandered in the direction of the old black building, he encountered on the way in. There certainly wasn't anything attractive about that place but it was oddly appealing in the way it stood its ground rebelliously imposing on the otherwise welcoming surroundings.

Steven was in the middle of ordering a plate of meatloaf when he was suddenly struck hard on the jaw sending him falling to the tiled floor. He was stunned. Managing to bring himself to his hands and knees, Steven looked down upon droplets of his blood straddling adjacent black and white tiles. He stood up on both knees and looked around to see who may have delivered the punch. The ambient sound of talking began to cease as everyone stopped to look at Steven. He saw the faces around the room and had a sense of déjà vu, remembering the day he fell hard from the windmill. As he touched the wet blood on his swelling lower lip, Steven rose to his feet. But as he was gathering his balance, his left foot rose from the floor and swiftly kicked against the lunch counter sending Steven airborne knocking over a table causing food, plates and silverware to crash on the floor.

A woman screamed.

Steven realized exactly what was happening. This was the moment he had feared and dreaded for years finally catching him by surprise in a full-scale blowout. There were no warnings, no stiffness in the arm or the impending sense of fear. This came out of nowhere and attacked him, blindsided him while he was far from being on guard. As he tried to bring himself to his feet, the assault came rapidly from his left fist pummeling his ear and the side of his face. Steven grunted as he grabbed his left wrist and desperately tried to wrestle it into submission. As he twisted and jerked in a bizarre dance, he tried to direct his body toward the door at the far end of the lunch counter. He attempted to move his feet but as he leaned forward to take a step, his left heal smashed down hard on the toes of his right foot causing him to scream in pain. Steven was down on the floor again, now trying to orient his weight against his left side while he continued to wrestle with his left arm. His feet were in a battle of one-upmanship resulting in an awkward pedaling motion. This continued for almost a minute as Steven became aware of the crowd cautiously surrounding him.

"Focus, be the laser beam," Steven forced himself to say through clenched teeth. But in this state of chaos and desperation, he couldn't break free from this struggle long enough to conjure up any kind of mental distraction. Then suddenly he became overwhelmed by the sound of his mother's voice, scalding him as though he had just been caught with his hand in his pants, "Steven!"

Upon hearing the startling shout of his name, the entire left side of Steven's body immediately became limp. Steven stood crouched on the checkered tile floor for a moment subconsciously trying not to be aware of the spectator's glaring eyes. Without giving it a second thought, Steven quickly jumped to his feet and lunged toward the door.

"Run", he said to himself as he pushed through two or three of his coworkers noticing Drake to his right with a scowl on his face. As he made a beeline toward the exit, he became aware of the searing pain that extended from his left calf muscle running up through his hip and back and outward past his left elbow. His head was numb. Now in a loping unstable gait, Steven was out of the cafeteria escaping from the embarrassing scene.

It wasn't until he made it to his Land Rover in the parking lot that Steven started to feel the panic lessen just a few degrees. Managing to get in the car and shut the door, he was out of breath. Steven sat for a minute or two with his eyes closed until he felt he was calm enough to start the engine and drive away. As he left the parking lot, he avoided looking back through his rear-view mirror.

Pain and stiffness shadowed the entire left side of his body as his head pounded with each heartbeat. Sweat was dripping down Steven's face mixed with blood from the cut under his left eye. He was trembling. His mind was blank as the drizzle of rain began to build on his windshield.

Steven drove for at least three miles before a thought finally surfaced in his head. He knew at that moment with absolute certainty that he would never ever return to his job. This assertion immediately brought about an image of his grandmother's expression of pity. Even though she had been buried long ago, it was difficult to push away memories of her disappointment in him as he now found himself struggling to move beyond an overwhelming feeling of shame.

Chapter 6

Steven's grandmother slipped on ice and died five days before her 70th birthday. It snowed four inches the night before her burial at Sheridan Hills Cemetery. Six months earlier in June, Steven moved out of her house and into his own apartment not more than six blocks away.

Grandma would have been very proud of Steven if she had lived long enough. She lived through the worst years of his childhood and then the long years of his recovery but didn't live long enough to see him succeed in having a seemingly normal life with a career, making a decent living. She wasn't a devout Christian but held onto a private faith left over from her Catholic upbringing. She tried to keep her prayers and her guilt to herself and never imposed her beliefs on anyone else. Steven's grandmother believed in the Devil, but nothing frightened her more than her grandson. It was obvious to her that something just wasn't right with Steven even when he was still in diapers. She constantly prayed that he would not turn out like his mother and took it upon herself to see that he was raised with the attention he needed.

"Grandma, why won't he close his eyes?"

Steven's grandmother was horrified one day to see him sitting on the ground next to a dead dog. The dog was positioned on its back with its head propped up on a shoe, so it appeared to be looking straight up. Steven was looking down into its eyes just a few inches away.

Did he kill the dog? How long had he been there gazing into those blank gray eyes? Steven was only 6 years old but didn't seem to care that flies were buzzing around his face. Grandma didn't overreact. She gathered her thoughts and decided not to make a big deal over this and hopefully help him gain a humane understanding of death. Steven's mother had already been committed to spending an eternity in the mental institute and Grandma feared for her grandson that he might follow in her footsteps. She needed to be delicate.

"The poor doggy's body remains here but his soul has left him," she said with a slight quiver. "His body is empty and sad without it and he wants it back so badly so he can live again. His eyes are still open because he's watching and waiting hoping for his soul to return."

As she was saying this to Steven, she was aware that it might sound a little bizarre even to an impressionable young boy. None the less, she set out to show Steven that death is a sad and tender time and should be confronted with respect and compassion. She opened her purse and dug out two coins and held them in the palm of her hand.

"I'll put pennies on his eyes," she said, "and all his sadness will go away." Pinching each eye closed, she put the pennies in place with the head side up sticking to the gooey eye secretions. Then she lightly patted the top of its head. "There you go, doggy. He's not sad anymore," she said. "Can you say goodbye to the doggy?"

"Bye-bye," Steven said quietly.

Grandma led Steven inside and parked him in front of the TV while she called animal control. When they arrived, she didn't go out to meet them but watched from inside, hidden behind a curtain.

Steven's mother died in the mental hospital when he was 8, the year before the accident. Both his behavior and his grades went downhill rapidly during this time. On more than a few occasions Grandma had to pick him up at school after he had thrown rocks at others on the playground. Apparently, the kids had made fun of his mother, and he would go ballistic.

But Grandma was always very patient with Steven. Where she lacked discipline, she made up for it in prayer. She prayed every day that her grandson would turn out to be normal and not have to live through the same nightmares as his mother. On the day of the windmill accident, she prayed. When she first arrived at the hospital after receiving the phone call from the police, Grandma prayed that Steven would die. Knowing his head had been split apart, she feared he would be conscious and in excruciating agony. This was something she would not be able to deal with; the idea of his brain being cut in half was almost enough to cause her to faint. She didn't expect him to ever recover. It was an enormous surprise when he was able to have a normal conversation with her only one week after the accident.

Unfortunately, the day of the accident was not the last of the horror Steven would bring into his grandmother's life. Even through her Pollyanna smile, nothing disturbed Grandma more than when Steven began to show signs of his sinister left hand. Her inner Catholic girl was convinced this was the work of the Devil, but she knew better and sought medical help. But the Doctors' explanations were complicated. All she understood was that Steven was increasingly developing a split personality as part of the separation of his brain. She was in denial that he was suffering from schizophrenia or whatever it was and refused to accept a long-term therapy plan for her grandson.

Grandma instead chose to continue praying. She spent hours with Steven every day helping him with school and praising every one of his accomplishments. She was bound and determined to bring him up to have a normal life though there were days when she lost her patience helping Steven to get past his episodes.

When he was a teenager, he would get angry and lash out at his left arm whenever it took its own direction. He would hit and even bite his hand until it went into submission. One time he even clamped his left hand to the arm of a chair out of frustration just to control it long enough to do his homework. Grandma nearly choked when she saw this. As he grew older, Steven realized he couldn't live his life fighting his left arm. The bully approach just seemed to make episodes more frequent and more violent.

By the time he was 20 years old, Steven learned he could control this other part of him by diversion. It came to him one day while watching a mother handle her young daughter in the grocery store where he worked. The little girl was upset about not getting any gum from the display at the checkout counter. The mother quickly abated the whining by feigning fascination over a tabloid newspaper picture of a monkey-faced space alien. The child was easily distracted, forgot about the gum and settled down. Steven learned from this that he could qualm his left hand by focusing his attention on something totally unrelated, specifically something that required some level of concentration such as a puzzle or a math problem.

Steven eventually became very intelligent, motivated entirely by day-to-day survival. When he felt the familiar stiffness in his left arm, he would immediately create a diversion of thought. It was the thought process that took hold of his brain and stifled the opposing force from within him. And just as the little girl in the grocery store could be diverted only once or twice by the monkey-alien, Steven found that he needed to constantly find new ways of mentally challenging himself. He directed his interests toward physics, electronics and software.

Ultimately, he was able to get a professional job in a software security firm which led to his position as a Systems Auditor in the corporate world.

Steven's ongoing intellectual pursuits during his mid-twenties also took him down the path of medical science. It was at this time that he stumbled across an explanation of his condition that both gave him comfort as well as frightened him to his core. SBD, Split Brain Disorder, the condition where the corpus callosum is damaged or severed preventing information to be shared between the two hemispheres of the brain.

Apparently, a mad doctor in the 1960's had severed the corpus callosum of epilepsy patients with some degree of success; the patients rarely had seizures as a result. However, a common side effect was that the patients had a second, darker identity they could not always control. Just as with Steven, these patients had a sinister left hand that would occasionally surprise them. Usually, this weird condition would be just a nuisance or a distraction but other times it could turn violent and destructive. One women patient was horrified by the act of her left hand as she was a witness and a participant in the strangling of her own cat.

A single brain split into two halves each with their own identity, personality, values and motivations. How could this be? This seemed to go against every intuitive sense of what consciousness meant. Even schizophrenics don't have simultaneous identities, they just flip from one channel to the next. As perplexing of an enigma that SBD presented, Steven gained a much better understanding of his condition. He realized that his darker side was just himself, the way he was before the windmill blade cut deep into his head, his child self he left behind that horrible day. He would have to live with the fact that he shared his mind with a parasite, a worm burrowing through the core of his brain.

Steven was almost 30 years old by the time he first visited his grandmother's grave. He had come a long way in bringing himself to a point where he could function in the world. Steven no longer denied who or what he was. His acceptance of self, or *selves*, finally allowed him to grieve for his long-gone grandmother. He didn't bring flowers to Sheridan Hills Cemetery that day. But without giving it any thought, Steven set two pennies on top of her gravestone.

Chapter 7

The nasal music from the AM band of the radio was just loud enough to drown out the sound of the car engine. The sounds from the Big Band era of the 1930s and 40s falsely conveyed the sense of happiness and celebration. The upbeat rhythms seemed contrived and forced. And the people of that time similarly appeared to not let on who they really were, nor did they reveal the obvious pain in their lives. As long as you danced along with the music and smiled predictably, everything was just ducky. Life was but a pathetic old black and white movie.

The reality of the outer world eventually crept back into Steven's mind once he realized he was almost out of gas. He had been aimlessly driving for four and half hours and his butt was sore. While filling his tank with high octane Texaco Premium he also realized he hadn't eaten any food since the nachos at the neighborhood party last night.

Oh yeah, the party. The little incident that turned out to be a mere catalyst foreshadowing today's epoch meltdown.

What was happening to me, Steven thought to himself as he pumped gas. The techniques he had perfected over the years suddenly seemed useless. His skills in the art of distraction had helped him inhibit his antagonistic other self enough to maintain an adequate level of self-control but what did it amount to now? Avoiding the problem didn't make it go away and certainly did not tame it. Instead, repressing it over the years apparently caused it to grow and fester until it just blew like a volcano. Steven conceded it was bound to happen sooner or later.

All those years of fooling myself into thinking I had the upper hand are wasted, Steven thought. His stomach sank as he realized he would be starting over from scratch. Not only would he need a new strategy for dealing with his mental problems, but he would also need to look for a new job. But maybe it was time to move on from his so-called career. He hated computers and hated pretending to fit in amongst the snooty engineers. The idea of never having to sit under those ridiculously bright office lights brought a half-smile to Steven's face.

While paying for the gas, Steven also purchased a Coke and six large candy bars, four of them were Snickers.

As he walked with a slight limp back to the Land Rover he thought about going home. But somehow the idea of being in his living room in front of his TV didn't bring him the regular feeling of security. Instead, he felt dread thinking about having to confront his neighbors who might have seen him run from the party last night. He would probably have to deal with the knucklehead ex-marine and his girlfriend, which could be enough to kick off yet another unexpected tantrum from his left side. Steven strapped on his seatbelt and began to drive. As he opened a candy bar wrapper, he decided he would instead head back to the old suburb on the west side of town for a return visit. Why not? He had all the time in the world now.

As he drove through the light rain it occurred to Steven that over the last ten minutes or so he had managed to turn his thoughts toward his future accepting the inevitable new challenges. He could have just as easily pulled over to the side of the road and curled up into a fetal position in the back seat, pouting until he starved to death. But instead, he was embracing change. This made Steven feel a lot better about himself. He almost dared to laugh at the events from earlier in the day but then thought better of it. He needed to move on, to reinvent himself.

Steven looked at his watch and noticed it was nearly five o'clock. Even though the sun had been hidden behind the rain all day it was noticeably getting darker. He wasn't exactly sure where he was, so he decided to pull over. He ripped open the last of the candy bars. By now he had to force down the chocolate, fighting the sickening sweet taste that had accumulated.

Steven decided to get out of the car and take in the quiet of the natural landscape on the edge of town. He allowed the cool moisture to build up on his swollen face as he crossed his arms and evaluated the reduction of leaves on the trees surrounding him. In a glimpse to the west, Steven was able to spot the top of the dark, imposing building peeking through the cottonwood trees a little more than two blocks away. The harsh right angles of the walls and the flat roof refreshed Steven's memory of the detour he took this morning. His curiosity piqued.

Steven was back in his car. Before he started the engine he leaned to his right and briefly glanced up at the rear-view mirror. He paused for a moment and then looked back up at the reflection of his dark, sagging eyes.

"Hell."

A few moments later the Land Rover pulled into the long drive that led to the front of the black building. Steven turned off the engine and sat quietly looking at it. It was a grim structure, cold and dreary. Just as he had observed earlier in the morning, the black building appeared uninhabited. Then he noticed there was a dim light emanating from a first-floor window. He looked for a moment but there were no signs of life. Wait, a shadow, or was that just my imagination, Steven thought. He stared into the window for a few more minutes. Nothing.

Without giving it a second thought, Steven got out of the car and began to walk toward the wood porch. He glanced into the window every few seconds. He stopped short of the porch and looked upward at the black cinder block wall with the tall narrow windows. From this close-up perspective he could see that the walls were not perfectly smooth but instead were roughly textured from erosion and then coarsely painted over. In two or three spots the cinder blocks had eroded enough to see a visible hole into the center cavity.

Looking back at his Land Rover, it seemed much farther away than the twenty or so steps he'd taken. He looked back to the window, still no movement. He noticed dead leafless vines clinging to the wall in sparse patterns. He followed the vines as they sprawled up to about the middle of the second floor. Steven looked back down at the window but quickly jerked his head upward when he thought he saw something fly out from one of the holes. Was that a bat?

"Can I help you?"

Steven just about jumped out of his skin. He looked up at the old man standing on the porch in front of the opened door. Staring blankly, he couldn't quite bring himself to say anything.

"Vwot are you doing here?" The old man had a big shaggy white mane of hair and a robust beard. He had big lips and a big nose and thick rimmed glasses that looked as though they were drawn on his face with a black marker.

"I... I'm sorry. I was driving... and... I was wondering what... I..."

The old man crooked his head to the left as he watched Steven stammer.

"I don't really know why I'm here." Steven blurted out. "I drove by here this morning... I've never seen this place before. I guess I'm just a little curious why this place is so... so freaking *creepy*."

To Steven's surprise the old man put his hands on his big round belly and began to laugh. His double chin was exaggerated by his oversized clown smile. Steven noticed how the old man stood in disproportion to his enormous round middle. He was an orb. The old man could probably roll faster than he could walk.

"Dis place it is so creepy because it has been condemned for many years. It vas once the Demszky Inn. I am Uri Demszky."

"Hello. I'm Steven. I'm sorry, I didn't mean to imply..."

"It was built by my father in 1943 while I was growing up in the western region of Hungary. He rented rooms here until he saved enough money to send for me and my brothers." The old man had a curious enthusiasm about him.

Uri stepped inside briefly and brought out a tall stool and set it next to the wood chair on the porch, welcoming him to take a seat. But Steven wasn't so sure he wanted to sit and chew the fat with old Uri. Even though he seemed friendly enough, he had the feeling that once the old man started talking, he might not stop. But the fascination of this building outweighed any of the usual anti-social excuses Steven could come up with. So, he sat on the stool towering over the round old man who sat below in the wood chair.

Much of what Uri had to say was worth listening to. The long overseas journey he and his two brothers took in the late 1950s, the day he took over the Demszky Inn, his three marriages, his father's death and on and on. Sometimes Uri was difficult to understand. As he would go on in his story telling, his words would occasionally fade into a kind of babble. Maybe someone who spoke Hungarian could make it out, but it mostly sounded like gibberish, "a-ga-dabba-ba-nabba-dadagah-badagabah." Then as Uri seemed to realize he was droning; he was back to speaking with regular volume using relatively understandable English.

Uri simply referred to the building as the Inn, apparently tired of repeating his own name over the years. He said that shortly after the building had been condemned, he stopped getting an electric bill although the Inn continued to receive power. Hence, he continued to use the building as his residence assuming the electric company would someday catch on, but they never did. Consumed in his one-sided conversation, Uri never bothered to ask why Steven's face was roughed up.

It was getting cold. Steven was wearing the sweater he wore to work but it had been dark for almost an hour and the temperature had dipped considerably. Uri must have noticed the chill as well and rose to his feet and held the door open for Steven. He reluctantly followed.

Standing inside the doorway, Steven sized up the Inn after just one sniff. It was musty and dank. It reminded Steven of an old automobile and train museum he visited last year where the years of dirt and oil on the machinery combined to leave a permanent membrane of odor throughout the exhibits.

A long counter stood beyond the facade of the Inn. A bare pegboard for the room keys was mounted to the wall next to a grid of empty mail slots. Steven half-expected to see a bell and a signature sheet sitting on the counter but it was also void of any objects.

To the left of the counter was a spacious parlor with rows of sofas and large chairs. Each was covered with a white sheet. The only exposed furniture in the room was a collection of end tables with various styles of lamps emanating a dirty yellowish glow through old lampshades. At the far end of the parlor, towards the back of the building, there was an entrance into an area where Steven could faintly make out a staircase in the shadows.

Even though the room was wide and consumed the better part of the first floor, Steven felt confined, almost claustrophobic. He realized this was because of the relatively low ceiling. There were water stains in some areas causing the drywall to slightly sag and the yellow light streaming up from the dilapidated lampshades gave the ceiling an overall blotchy appearance.

Uri graciously offered a covered chair to Steven. At first a bit reticent, Steven sank down into the big cushions feeling his body go limp with relaxation. It had been a long draining day. Even though this place gave Steven the creeps, sitting in this dreary Inn listening to an old Hungarian was a welcome removal from the reality of his bad day. As Uri sat across from Steven on a covered sofa, he continued to go on about life in America with his two brothers and three lost wives. Occasionally as Uri faded into a quiet mumble, Steven would prod him with a pointless question bringing Uri back to the present.

It wasn't long before Steven found himself fading from the conversation. He continued to glance and nod at Uri but was mostly preoccupied with the interior of the parlor. He was startled when he briefly saw the silhouette of a small boy sitting at the bottom of the staircase beyond the doorway at the end of the room. As soon as he jerked his head in the direction of the staircase, the boy was gone. It was more like an image from a hologram than a silhouette as the kid only seemed to appear when seeing it at a certain angle. Looking back at Uri, Steven sensed the boy sitting on the stairs using his periphery vision from his left eye. As soon as he looked directly towards the stairs, it would disappear. Steven wasn't sure if this was his imagination catching up to him, but he distinctly sensed he was being watched. He could feel it in his bones.

Vaguely listening to Uri go off into another rant of undecipherable mumbling, Steven closed his eyes. He feared that if he were to let the creepiness of this building get to him, he might let his guard down and allow his sinister side to bring on yet another attack.

But he was just too exhausted to do anything about it. Since it had come to mind, Steven could feel the subtle presence inside of him. He sensed it coyly watching from the corner of his mind, ready to strike at any moment. But instead of fighting it or trying to avoid it, he cautiously let it surface within him out of passive curiosity. Steven concentrated on being calm and paid attention to his breathing. He could sense its reluctance to just come out of the shadows of his mind after all the years of contention and suppression. After all, extending an open invitation to his life's foe wasn't something he ever thought he would do, and it likely didn't expect this either. And at first it was awkward. It wasn't so much a matter of consciously yielding to it but mostly just having an open mind and giving it an opportunity to co-exist. To Steven's surprise, this started to feel right. He felt he might be able to allow both of his extreme personalities to share his mental space although he knew he may be putting himself at risk of another meltdown.

Staying calm and continuing to keep his eyes closed, Steven let himself feel what his other self was feeling. It was somewhat a feeling of bashfulness but mostly curiosity. Steven was almost delighted to be sharing this childish pique of interest. He was so consumed by this revelation that he completely lost sight of Uri's ongoing monologue. He sat in the comfortable chair with his eyes closed keenly aware of his child-self coming out of the closet with trepidation. He noticed his left hand had lightly touched the side of his face with zero aggression. This was the answer. This was how he was going to cope with his debilitating mental condition going forward. Steven smiled as the lyrics of an old "War" song came to mind, "Why can't we be friends, why can't we be friends...." Steven was pleased with this new sense of confidence. He considered how different things might have been if he had figured this out years ago.

Uri continued to drone on not really caring that his unexpected visitor was falling asleep. He noticed Steven had a slight, yet crooked smirk that began to fade to an expression of content. After a few minutes, Steven started snoring.

Chapter 8

N orman sat on the staircase staring toward the front of the parlor. He had no idea how long he'd been there or where he had been before.

The building was quiet.

Earlier Norman had noticed the front door open briefly and then shut again. He had been sitting and staring with mild anticipation that sooner or later it would open back up. He remained completely still except when he touched the gashes on his face.

Norman faded briefly. But almost as fast as his light had dimmed, Norman was struck back to awareness as a faint glow in the parlor caught his attention. As he regained his focus the glow disappeared. So, he sat and stared toward the front of the parlor. Waiting....

Then, in the distance of the long room, two red dots emerged but immediately faded away. Now at least he knew where to focus his attention. It was just a matter of staring at that point in space until it returned. Norman was captivated but patient.

Before long the two red dots appeared again toward the front of the parlor. This time there was an odd amber glow surrounding the dots. Norman strained to make out the shape of this unusual aura. The two dots coalesced into one and seemed to be swallowed within the amber shape as the glowing blob lacked any distinct lines of contour.

Norman continued to stare until the red dots abruptly appeared again, but this time it was clear that the amber mass had structure and deliberate movement. The red dots disappeared again as the image seemed to turn away. Now it was becoming obvious that the amber glow was in the shape of a body as Norman stared at its emerging profile. It was the head and shoulders of a person. The outline of a nose, mouth and chin became apparent with an ear that had a lighter golden tone below what looked to be a crew-cut haircut with curtain-rod bangs.

Norman realized this was an animated image of a boy his age that he was staring at. And, apparently, it was also interested in him as it seemed to be glancing in his direction. The form was still vague but seemed to be building density as Norman continued staring at it. Intrigued, he needed a closer look. Before he was even aware of his intention to stand up and walk into the parlor, Norman found himself standing directly behind the amber boy looking down upon him. He stared with curiosity.

The amber boy sat back in the large old chair with his eyes closed facing upward. Was it alive? Where did it come from? The smooth contours of the glowing face gave way to the subtle light emanating from within.

Norman stood there, looking down over the top of the chair, staring into the boy's transparent face waiting for him to open his eyes. He wanted to see the blazing red eyes again. He wanted to feel the energy he sensed from within this strange outsider. Norman waited impatiently leaning over the boy's forehead. Before long he was only a few inches from the translucent amber face meeting eye to opposite eye, waiting, staring.

The anticipation was killing Norman. Unable to contain himself, he leaned closer to within an inch of the amber boy's face and then let out a long, loud, horrific scream.

Chapter 9

Steven slowly came to, woken by the sound of dripping water. His first realization was that he wasn't in his bed. He had no sense of the time of day or where he could possibly be.

I must be sleepwalking, he considered.

His head was pounding. He allowed himself to slowly come to his senses and to assess the matter before he would open his eyes. Over the years he trained himself well to take his time, coming to terms with a potentially bad situation before resorting to panic.

Steven listened to water dripping. Slow repetitive drops of water fell from a distance of at least a few feet as the high-pitched plops revealed. There was a second drip coming from the same area. This one was much less frequent and had a lower pitch. The slight echo convinced him that he was indoors. Steven was lying on his back on a hard cold cement floor. It didn't feel wet though there was obviously water nearby.

He felt he had enough of his wits about him to open up his eyes and face whatever he had gotten himself into. As he slowly sat up, he realized his eyes were already open. It was completely dark. Keeping his mind and his imagination from racing, he sat motionless in the pitch black trying to recount the steps that led him here. Slowly the recollection of his meltdown at work surfaced. He thought about the party, the oriental palm reader, the dunderhead ex-marine. He remembered Uri.

Was he still in that odd black building the fat old Hungarian called the Inn?

Steven rose to his feet. Feeling lightheaded, he took a few breaths and tried to orient himself in the dark. He slowly took a few steps along the wall but only made it a few feet before he hit his head on something hard. Steven gathered he had walked into a metal pipe by the low pinging sound it produced. He paused and regained his calm before attempting to make another move.

The prospect of having a sheer panic attack was looming. Got to stay cool, got to keep control, he told himself. He sensed the presence of his other self as though it was watching from a distance but that wasn't something to be concerned about right now. Just focus on finding a way out.

Steven moved against the wall in the other direction. He listened to the exaggerated sound of his shoes shuffling across the smooth floor. After five steps he encountered a corner of the room. He continued to follow the wall to his left continuously feeling the surface with his hand.

Eventually Steven had worked his way to the opposite side of the room. He felt a door jamb. He quickly moved his hands over the surface of the door until he found the knob. It wouldn't turn. He instinctively put his left hand on the wall next to the door and felt a light switch. Upon flipping the switch, the room burst into a brief explosion of blue florescent light and again went dark. A moment passed and then the light burst on again. This time it remained illuminated. Steven was relieved to be back in a world of vision but was no less confused by where he found himself. Looking around his dank surroundings, he realized he was in a utility room where a large boiler occupied most of the space. It didn't appear that it had been used for years. Next to the boiler were a washer and dryer standing side by side. Steven noticed a trap door on the ceiling above and to the side of the appliances, probably a clothes chute.

Ten or more chrome pipes were fed into this room from the ceiling and from two of the four walls. Apparently, these were drainpipes as each had a U-shaped catcher piece. The mesh of pipes gave an overall appearance of a twisted, busy network. Each of the drainpipes, as well as the washing machine drain hose, connected to a larger copper pipe that directed the water through the floor and apparently out to the sewer. All the pipes were overly shiny. Someone must've loved this menagerie of metal and spent time polishing the pipes until they reflected like mirrors.

Steven looked down at the locked doorknob and noticed smudges all over the door as well as on the light switch. He looked at his left hand and noticed it was moist and sticky with a brownish substance. It wasn't just on his hand as Steven saw that he had softball sized spots on his sweater as well.

It was blood.

Looking down his shoes and lower pant-legs were soaking red. He noticed the path of his bloody footprints from the door to the other side of the room where he created a small puddle from lying on the floor. The blood trail, albeit much fainter, continued along the wall to the position he currently stood. Alongside the footprints were crimson spots that apparently dripped from his hand.

It was time to take inventory. Am I hurt? Am I losing blood? After a few minutes Steven concluded the blood wasn't his. Other than his headache and bruised face he was not injured. How long have I been here?

"Hellooo," Steven scared himself by the sheer emptiness of his small voice in this dungeon of a room. He again tried to turn the doorknob. As he looked down, he was relieved to see that the door was locked from the inside. He wasn't a prisoner after all.

Why in the world would I lock myself in this room? He wondered.

Steven felt a surge of hunger. He was so dry he could barely swallow. His mouth tasted acidic like he had been sucking on old nails. He was weak and woozy, but he knew he needed to gather his energy and get out. He took a deep breath.

As he began to twist the doorknob lock, Steven sensed that he was not alone. Out of the periphery of his left eye he noticed a shadow moving in the corner under the bulk of the pipes. Not wanting to look at what was there Steven quickly turned the knob and yanked the door wide open. But before he could move forward out into the hallway, the door ripped out of his hands and slammed shut. Steven stood motionless, petrified from the unexpected force of the door.

He started to reach for the doorknob but stopped when he felt the hair on the back of his neck rise. He reluctantly moved his head to the left and slowly looked over his shoulder. The shadow was gone. But as Steven looked toward the array of pipes he froze as he noticed a pair of bulging bloodshot eyes staring at him. The eyes seemed to be floating, just hanging in midair. Steven blinked trying to flush the illusion but now he saw many sets of eyes all staring at him. It was the pipes. The pipes were all projecting large, sad and glassy gray eyes staring right at him. The disembodied eyes, reflections or otherwise, caused Steven to stiffen with fear. A wave of goose bumps rushed down his spine leaving him unable to do much more than emit a quivering cry of fear though it was barely audible. He stood motionless for another few seconds but then Steven knew he had to either move quickly or risk succumbing to the terror and possibly having another attack.

Suddenly the light went out and it was pitch dark again. The florescent light rapidly flashed on and off making a crackling sound. For a split second, Steven saw the big bulging eyes again but this time they were embedded in the battered face of a little boy sitting on the floor. He sat holding his knees to his chest looking up at Steven with an evil grin. He had the freakish appearance of one of those hideous wind-up toy monkeys that would smile and bang a pair of cymbals.

Steven must have managed to get through the door because he found himself blindly running as fast as he could down a dimly lit hallway. He figured he was in a basement but had no idea which way was out. Steven stopped running about twenty feet short of the end of the hall when he realized the only exit in this direction was a closed door. Looking back at the way he had come, he could not see the other end as it faded into the dark. He noticed the faint bloody footprints he just made on the cement floor when running to this end of the hall, but there were no other tracks. He must have come into the basement from the other side of the utility room. Steven looked down the hall again into the dark. He could tell the utility room door was open and the light was still on. He stood for a moment, catching his breath and collecting his thoughts. Were there stairs at that end of the building? He had shuddered at the thought of having to go back down the hall past the utility room.

Listening, Steven could only hear his rapid heartbeat from his throbbing temples. Do I want to try the door at this end of the hall or make a run to the other side?

Instead, Steven didn't do anything but remain petrified with his back against the wall.

"I'm just seeing shit" he said softly, trying to calm down. The little boy with the cut-up face had to be his imagination.

Steven swallowed hard and gritted his teeth. Looking down at the floor he took a step in the direction he had come from and paused to shake the chill out of his shoulders. Before he began to walk back down the hallway, he suddenly had a change of heart and pivoted on his left foot and turned 180 degrees. If the other end of the hall was a dead end, then he didn't want to have to pass the utility room again to get back here. As he approached the only door at the end of the hallway, he considered knocking but the thought that someone might be down here gave him the creeps. He quickly turned the doorknob expecting the door to be locked. Instead, it opened with ease. The light from the hanging bulb in the hallway illuminated enough of the room that Steven could tell it was used for storage. He quickly scanned the shapes and shadows and could make out an old sowing machine, appliances, shelves of books, broken tables and chairs and piles of clothes. Was that a mannequin?

Without hesitation Steven closed the door. It wasn't an exit so there was no need to turn on the light and go in and poke around. The fact of the matter was that this room looked a lot scarier than the utility room. He turned and looked back down the hall. He knew he could sprint to the other side but decided it would be best to try and control himself and hopefully keep a lid on his fear. He started walking.

The florescent light from the utility room emanated a dingy glow into the hallway. As Steven came closer to the partially opened door, he became aware of the faint sound of the dripping water. When he was within ten feet of the door, he could see into the room far enough to glimpse into the corner under the pipes where he had seen the weird kid. He relaxed just a notch when he verified for himself that nothing was there. He must have imagined it all. Steven let out an overdue breath.

As he walked past the door, he gave the utility room a passive glance expecting to see nothing. Again, he was relieved the room was empty. He cursed himself for having to look twice.

Now that Steven was beyond the glow from the utility room he could faintly make out an opening at the end of the hall. It was too dark to see into the entry but at least this was encouraging. He looked down and saw the bloody footprints he made apparently from when he initially fled to the utility room. What in the world was I doing, Steven mused. He raised his bloody hands in front of his face intentionally reminding himself that something was seriously wrong, and he was a world away from his usual crappy life.

A faint whisper seeped from the utility room, "Steeee-ven."

Stopping in his tracks, Steven deliberately avoided believing he really heard that. Listening intently from the hallway he heard only the faint sound of the dripping and realized it was practically in sync with his heart. As he began walking, he heard it again.

"Steeeeeeee-ven"

Is someone calling me? I heard my *name*. Steven was acutely aware of his other self, perking up in response to the eerie voice that seemed to reverberate from the utility room pipes. He didn't entertain the idea of turning around. Instead, he bolted down the corridor where he could make out the lower two steps from a stairway peering out from the opening at the end of the hall.

He quickly plunged upward on the cement steps using his hands and feet as assurance he wouldn't trip. It was dark, the stairwell was not lit. As he lurched up the first flight of steps, Steven noticed a yellowish-brown light coming from beyond the next flight. He was making a wheezing, shrieking sound as he turned the corner, gasped for air. As he approached the top of the steps, he slowed his pace to a walk. Standing upright and holding onto the narrow banister, Steven's attention was focused on the room beyond the small outlet at the top of the steps. He paused, pulling together his composure trying to breathe normally. He stood looking forward, choosing not to look back down the stairs.

Steven recognized the parlor where he had previously fallen asleep while listening to the fat Hungarian. This wasn't a big surprise since he suspected he had been in the basement of the Inn. He also wasn't too shocked when he looked around the room. He more than half-expected to encounter exactly what he was seeing in front of him. It was a freaking blood bath.

Chapter 10

The surrealism of the gore splattered parlor made Steven swoon slightly. Standing with both hands loosely hanging to his sides, he chose not to lean against the wall for support. Instead, he stiffened his wobbling knees and tried to force himself to calm down.

Surveying the large room, he was overcome by all the dots, hundreds of red dots everywhere. The floor beneath his red feet and the low ceiling above him were spotted with blood. The sheets covering the furniture nearest Steven displayed sparsely distributed droplets but a few of the sheets toward the front of the parlor had large areas completely doused in red. The wall to the left had become a mural of a red tidal wave complete with a lunging half-pipe cap.

What in the world could have happened?

After a moment of acclimation from the initial shock, Steven looked toward the front of the parlor at the door just beyond the facade. He thought about his four-wheel drive parked out in the mud and considered his escape route through the parlor. He continued to look around the room. Other than the mass amounts of blood everything seemed to be in order. No broken lamps or misplaced sheets. He noticed bloody footprints a few feet beside him heading in the opposite direction. Recognizing they were his own, he again looked at his sticky crimson hands, perplexed.

He stood perfectly still, aware that whoever did this might still be the parlor somewhere. Listening for the slightest hint of the presence of some insane ax wielding maniac, Steven glanced around the room looking for any sign of movement. Only silence. But he had to be prepared. If he tried to run through the parlor someone might be waiting behind one of the sofas ready to pounce.

Crouching slightly and raising his hands in a pseudo-karate defense pose, Steven began to follow his own bloody footprints towards the front of the parlor. Moving around the first covered sofa, he looked down toward the check-in. The old wood floor was wet with blood, the light glinting off of something stringy in the center of the long streak. Steven didn't want to walk through the gore but was wary of walking between the covered sofas and chairs. He didn't want to turn his back on any potential hiding places where someone could jump him.

Then Steven remembered his frightful experience in the basement and realized his back was to the stairs.

Quickly he looked behind him, but no one was there. The stairs he had just run up were empty. Looking at the dark flight of stairs leading to the second floor, he remembered seeing the spooky little boy sitting there where he was listening to Uri.

Steven put it together. The dark image of the little boy he had seen earlier on the stairs must have been the same demonic looking kid he encountered in the basement. Could that little bastard have been responsible somehow for this bloody mess? No, he was just an illusion, a product of overwhelming stress. Or maybe a delusion as a result of deteriorating sanity. Steven didn't want to go there.

He cautiously started to move toward the front door and suddenly became acutely aware that he was humming to himself. It was just barely audible above each exhalation but there it was. Surprised by his own strange behavior, Steven held his breath. This apparently frustrated his child self which caused him to air the goofy tune loudly inside his head instead.

It was back again, sharing the occupation of his mind. His latest approach to dealing with it seems to have taken hold and it wasn't something Steven wanted to challenge at this time. He opened the gate, and it was probably best that he committed to sticking with it instead of trying to fight it. He had to try looking at this situation from a whole new perspective. Instead of an enemy, Steven could treat this newfound relationship as one with a sibling. A brother. A little buddy maybe. But after all of these years he knew it would be impossible to consider that little shit a friend. It was a parasite. A horrible little worm that infested his head as though it was a rotten apple.

Steven looked down at the chair he had sat in earlier listening to Uri babble on. This is where he deliberately coaxed his immature sinister side to come forward. He didn't want to acknowledge it but that was about the time when he blacked out. Ignoring the tune in his head, Steven put his attention back on the front door. It couldn't be more than twenty paces away; you just must get past the puddle of blood between here and there.

It occurred to Steven that the song in his head had quieted somewhat once he had focused his attention on the task at hand. It was as though *the worm* was creating a distraction avoiding having to face the horror show he was experiencing in the parlor. For so many years Steven had toiled over and perfected the ability to create a mental distraction to avoid his inner foe but now it seems just the opposite was happening.

Steven couldn't help but be grossed out by the sound of his steps sticking to the thick layer of blood on the floor. He deftly avoided the meaty chunks and continued to glance around the room. As Steven approached the check-in counter, he looked toward the door and saw a big round mound piled on the floor. It was the fat belly of the old Hungarian. What else could it be? Once Steven was close enough to the body, he could see that Uri was lying on his back with his legs and arms sprawled. He was covered in blood and had created a large pool around him. A bloody sheet was twisted over his head and shoulders. Steven felt his stomach rise into his throat. The last thing he wanted to do was barf, but it seemed inevitable.

The dorky music inside Steven's head was getting loud again. He knew that he would have to move Uri's corpse out of the way to be able to open the front door. But Steven was squeamish. It seemed like an impossible feat to move a dead body, let alone to touch one. He looked at the black shoes on his tiny feet and figured they would easily slip off so he would have to grab Uri by the ankles and pull him two or three feet away from the door. This wasn't going to be easy.

As Steven bent down and reached out toward Uri's leg, he noticed how badly his hand was shaking. Unable to swallow he tried to compose himself, but that stupid music wasn't helping. Steven accidentally touched Uri's shoe and his foot made an awkward yet slight movement. Chills bolted up Steven's spine and caused his shoulders to shiver. The stiffness and cold of death made a surprising and unsettling impression on him. The taste of old nails returned. Steven tried to be strong but found that he was crumbling from the weight he was putting on his bent knees and ankles.

I've got to do this, he demanded. Starting to feel angry he shouted in his head to stop that crappy music. To his surprise, the music in his head subsided. Without hesitation Steven knelt and grabbed both of Uri's ankles, got up on his feet and quickly jerked backward. Uri did not easily yield his position. Steven expected that he weighed at least a ton but didn't consider he would be stuck to the floor in his drying blood. Not about to give up, Steven wrenched Uri's body to the left and then to the right, freeing him up enough to try another yank. This time Uri gave a little ground, maybe four inches. He really did weigh a ton.

One... Two... Three... another jerk backward. This time he gave up a good foot and a half. Uri's belly rolled from the momentum. Steven had to give it just one more effort. Just as he was mustering the strength, Steven noticed the blood-soaked sheet beyond Uri's huge belly was caught on something and pulled away from the corpse's head. Steven quickly looked away. He didn't want to see what was under that sheet. He yanked at Uri's legs without looking up and found he was in a struggle to move the body any further. Twisting Uri to his right, Steven partially rolled the body off the floor. After a bit of struggling, Steven was able to get it to roll on its side. That should be good enough.

Steven stood up. Still looking away from Uri's face, he took a slow but deliberately large step over Uri's legs. He reached for the doorknob as he straddled the body. Just as he felt the cold metal in the palm of his hand Uri flopped onto his back again blocking the door with his shoulder and plump arm. Steven stepped back away from the sloshing corpse and without thinking about it looked toward Uri's face. His head was gone. Uri had been decapitated. All that remained was a stub of spine and shards of flesh. Blood was oozing freely in reaction to the movement.

Steven spun his entire body away from Uri as he collapsed to his knees. He started puking. Rapidly heaving, nothing was being expelled although a small amount of stomach acid was pumped into his mouth. Steven's diaphragm was aching. He clutched at his belly as he realized he was kneeling in a warm puddle of Uri's blood. This sickened him even more, preventing him from being able to get up. He was shaking badly. For now, he just wanted to be sure he kept breathing. And this turned out to be a difficult task. He tried to get a hold of himself, but he just went into another bout of dry heaves.

After a few minutes he managed to pull himself to his feet, crawling up the side of the check-in counter. At least he was standing again, sort of. Steven let out a groan and held his gut with both hands. His knees were shaking. He steadied himself by putting his elbow on the countertop then wiped his mouth with the other arm.

He didn't want to look back at Uri, he'd seen enough. Instead, he looked around and noticed to the side of the mail slots was a door, probably an office. Lying next to the door on the floor was a shovel. It had two distinct blood spots in the middle and at the end of the long wooden handle. Steven looked at his hands. He looked back at the shovel and could see chunks of hair and skin and other gore clustered near the tip of the head. Steven stood dumbfounded looking at the shovel. He tried to remember what had happened before he blacked out but drew a blank. He remembered Uri going on and on and how comfortable and relaxing the overstuffed chair felt. He remembered seeing the boy sitting on the stairs. Steven quickly looked toward the back of the parlor, but the demon child wasn't there. He recalled his newfound truce with his other self, the worm, and how he felt it come out and "smell the coffee" so to say.

Steven stared at the shovel. There was something magnetic about it, something alluring. The music in Steven's head roared to life again. What was the worm reacting to? It clouded Steven's thinking. Feeling impatient, Steven once again shouted internally to himself to shut up. The music abruptly stopped.

Without even giving it a thought, Steven picked up the shovel and was immediately overwhelmed with regret for doing so. He wanted to drop it but couldn't. He uncontrollably clutched it tightly. Part of him wanted this shovel in almost an addictive way. It felt right and felt a part of him. Steven tasted the acid in his mouth and grimaced. He wrestled with the handle until he finally managed to throw the shovel down. It clanged loudly on the wood floor.

"Oh my God," Steven whispered.

Steven stood silent amassing what had just happened. He could vaguely sense the worm in his brain as if it were saying, "you asked for it." He searched his mind. He looked for anything, a hint, a clue, a detached recollection of what might have happened earlier in the parlor. Steven was at a loss. Could he really have flipped out and hacked away at old Uri until he completely removed his head? "Oh my God," Steven repeated.

Steven had the intuitive sense that the music in his head was about to kick in again. He cut it off before it started by concentrating... "What do you know, what do you know, what do you know...." He whispered repeatedly hoping to gain some insight into the ordeal he found he was in. He increasingly felt the presence of the worm inside his head, and he could tell it was afraid. And why not, Steven himself couldn't recall a time in his life when he was more terrified. He dared him to come forward, to reveal something, anything. He waited and listened.

"C'mon," Steven prodded. He reached down and picked up the shovel, holding it upright like a rifle. And then the images came to him almost in a flood. He stiffened from the recollection of the thrashing and the swinging. He could feel the horizontal arc of the shovel and the subsequent force of the blow; the exhilaration and the hatred and the redemption all rolled up in a single adrenaline rush of violence. He wanted Uri dead beyond anything he had ever wanted before. He needed him to be dead. Needed him to be terminated, eliminated... beheaded!

The taste of acid wasn't from the bile in his mouth. It was lust, blood lust. His other self, the sinister self that he had insistently suppressed over all these years simply took over his consciousness and destroyed a man's life. Over years of having various levels of self-attacks and meltdowns, never has Steven blacked out and yielded full control over to it. Maybe his new approach to dealing with the entity wasn't such a great idea after all. Steven sunk a little when he realized this isn't something he might even have any control over. He was sharing his head with someone else, someone that was just him from another time, a forgotten past. But Steven had to deal with the reality that inside of him was a monster, a killer. This was a facet of himself he could not fathom. Yet Steven tasted it, the primal hatred and belligerence. He had glimpsed what it was like to savor the bludgeoning of an enemy. But why did he have so much hatred for Uri?

The weird demon boy was standing at the end of the parlor, staring. Steven froze and dropped the shovel. He slowly took a step backward but stopped short of stepping on Uri. It wasn't just a brief image between blinks, this time the boy was just standing there, staring at him from the parlor entrance by the stairs. Neither moved a muscle, they just gazed at each other over the distance of the room. Steven looked at the scrawny boy with a small sense of puzzling interest but mostly he felt the numbing electricity of fear. This didn't seem like an illusion or his imagination.

Steven heard a noise behind him. Reluctant to take his eyes away from the demon child he glanced over his shoulder, but he quickly looked back down the parlor thinking the apparition might be advancing. The big, piercing eyes of the boy continued to stare from across the room. Steven paused for a moment and heard more rustling behind him. This time he took a few more seconds to see what was going on. The headless body of the fat old Hungarian began to roll over. Steven stepped back. At first, he thought someone had opened the door pushing the body out of the way but then he saw something that caused him to become instantly paralyzed. Uri was pushing himself up on his knees. His short fat arms barely long enough to extend past his bloated belly shifted his weight onto his rear quarters. The headless Uri was trying to get up. The blood drained out of Steven's face. He strained but couldn't move a muscle. He would have wet himself if he hadn't been so dehydrated. Uri, prone on his hands and knees, began to turn and crawl toward Steven.

"No... No." Steven whimpered helplessly.

The paralysis finally snapped. Steven jerked away from the headless orb of terror and took three small steps backward towards the counter. But before he knew it, he fell hard on his butt, feet tripping over the shovel handle. Panicking, Steven didn't bother getting back on his feet; instead, he pushed off the floor with his knees and tried to squirm his way behind the counter. He lost his balance, slipping on the bloody floor falling hard on his hip. He struggled to get a grip on the floor with his shoes trying disparately to at least get back up on his knees. Then he suddenly felt his left leg slip out from under him. Uri had a hold of his ankle.

Steven squealed.

He grabbed the side of the counter and tried to pull away but the grip on his ankle was too tight. He knew he had to fight himself free but wasn't able to pull himself away. He was terrified of looking down. He simply did not want to acknowledge what was happening. Steven frantically began kicking with his free leg connecting with the stiff hand attached to his ankle. It wasn't budging. He also managed to kick Uri's other hand as it was feeling its way around for a second grip. Steven had to do something, anything. He considered the shovel which was somewhere on the floor off to his left. He held tight onto the base of the counter with one hand and attempted to reach the shovel with the other, patting a semicircle on the floor but unable to find it. Glancing down he saw the shovel about a foot out of his reach. He knew he would need to sit up to grab it which meant letting go of the counter. Before he could begin to make a move, his free leg suddenly was being yanked. Both ankles were now being clutched tightly by the headless Hungarian.

Steven began thrashing on the floor trying to break the grip. He twisted his body causing him to cross his legs, enabling him to pivot on his butt. An unintentional glimpse confirmed his nightmare was real. Uri was teetering on his bloated belly with arms outstretched pulling his bloody corpse closer. Uri reached up and advanced his grip onto Steven's knee causing a pain to shoot up his leg.

Steven let go of the counter and quickly made a move to retrieve the shovel. But as he sat up and started to lunge to his side, he found himself face to face, eye to eye with that freaky little demon boy.

Once again, Steven was paralyzed with fear.

Chapter 11

Norman was astonished to find himself nose to nose with the elusive amber specter, eyes aflame, locked in an impromptu staring contest. From the wild dance earlier right here in the parlor to the surprise appearance in the basement under the pipes, here it was, close enough to taste.

He slowly raised his long floppy left hand and moved it up toward the face of the glowing apparition, feeling the warmth. With his crooked index finger, he directly touched one of its red-hot eyes. Even with a finger buried in its eye, it remained in a locked gaze. Norman flinched at the onset of an electrical surge and retracted his finger. But he wasn't discouraged by the jolt. He slowly returned his hand, this time cupping his palm over the amber thing's cheek. Norman expected the heat and welcomed it.

To his delight, the amber boy began to glow brighter than ever. He heard a faint sound of thumping in the room but would not veer his attention to see what it was. Time and time again Norman found himself on the brink of closing in on this mysterious illumination only to slip away into his usual void. He wasn't going to let that happen this time. He continued to stare intently into its smoldering red eyes.

The thumping grew louder as the warmth increased in Norman's palm. Then he realized what was making the sound. He slowly looked down to find a brilliant reddish-purple jerking blob within its chest. It was pounding with urgency. Norman began drooling realizing an almost forgotten sensation…. hunger.

Stretching his thin lips back, showing his tiny, evenly spaced teeth, Norman wanted only to bury his face into this thing's heart. He opened his mouth as wide as possible. With the anticipation of a cobra, he cocked his head back ready to strike with every ounce of energy he could muster up.

But then Norman saw it. He dropped his left hand limply down to his side as his jaw went slack. He couldn't believe what he was looking at. On the floor, teetering on his fat belly was a man. With his arms outstretched, slightly kicking his legs into the air, he had Norman's prey in his grip.

Just who the hell was this intruder and where the hell was his head?

Chapter 12

No breath. Numbness. Vertigo. Fading...

The lights were going out on Steven. He was passively falling into darkness but managed to remind himself that he always knew he would someday die a bizarre death. His senses were still alive enough to feel the ice cold bolt of electricity that pierced through his right eye. The pain streaked down the side of his face and into his jaw. He was frozen stiff and there was nothing he could do to defend himself.

Steven was aware of his child half, the worm, and its own astonishment with this ghostly encounter. With regret, Steven felt the impending loud music about to flare up once again. Lacking any strength, he couldn't fight it. He just stood there sitting upright, completely paralyzed. One final statement I suppose, he thought to himself.

To Steven's surprise, it wasn't the stupid music that took over in his head. Instead, it was something else. It was that tantalizing rush he had felt when he previously held the shovel. Hatred. Rage. He felt his heart begin to pound and his blood surge. Steven clenched his teeth hard tasting the old nails again. He narrowed his vision to the point of squinting still feeling the icy heat from the intrusive poke in the eye. He looked at the evil little boy in front of him with disdain and noticed that his attention had wandered down to the Hungarian.

With both fists, Steven rammed the demon child square in his chest as hard as he could. He half expected to only feel air, still not quite certain that what was confronting him was real. But he connected. He sent the squirrelly, wild-eyed kid flying backward, tumbling out of sight behind a covered sofa.

Thump! Suddenly the back of Steven's head hit the floor hard and bounced slightly. The Hungarian had yanked his legs sending him flat on his back. But this only added to Steven's adrenaline rush. Clenching his fists, he growled at the ceiling. He began kicking and thrashing, trying to squirm himself free. He still couldn't budge the tight grip around his ankle and his knee, but he was causing Uri to rock wildly on his fat belly.

Steven sat up and lunged for the shovel again. This time reaching out and grabbing it while looking down and noticing the hideous piece of spine protruding from Uri's former neck. Realizing he had grabbed the shovel from the wrong end, Steven awkwardly swung the long end of the handle. He hit arms and elbows but couldn't strike with enough force to evoke any sign of submission. Frustrated, Steven put his weight back on his elbows and arched his back trying to gain some leverage. He managed to separate his legs causing Uri's fat arms to spread outward. Steven peered down into the slight opening of Uri's esophagus.

Without any forethought of what he'd do next, Steven took the shovel with both hands and shoved the handle straight down Uri's throat. It penetrated about a foot deep into his body. Steven hesitated for only a moment and then pushed the handle down further with a hard thrust. He felt it rip through the inner guts of the fatso. Pulling himself closer by bending his knees, he pushed on the shovel again until it stopped deep within Uri's bowels. Steven all at once felt both disgust and morbid delight. Uri finally let go of Steven's legs.

Steven quickly got up on his feet. He was invigorated with new hope, new energy. Uri, teetering on his belly, reached up and grabbed at the head of the shovel, which was sticking out about a foot above his shoulders. Losing his balance, he attempted to get on his knees as he tried to push the shovel out. Instead, he fell forward slumping down with the tip of the shovel touching the floor.

Steven reacted quickly, taking one step forward and raising his right foot in the air. He slammed down his heel with force onto the wooden handle. Crack! It splintered. Steven slammed his foot down again. This time the shovel head broke free and clanged on the floor with a dull clunk. A pointed shard of wood about five inches long was all that remained in lieu of Uri's head.

Steven stepped back and leaned against the check-in counter, panting. His eyes shimmered from the craziness. His hands started shaking, then his knees. He surprised himself. He was in awe of himself.

Uri, back to teetering on his belly, struggled with the stub of wood. It was wedged tight and wouldn't budge. After a few moments he gave up and redirected his efforts to getting himself on his knees. He unexpectedly managed to get a foot up on the floor by burying his knee into his bloated belly. Then he straightened up his torso. And there he was, standing erect, hands proudly resting on his round middle.

Steven quickly shuffled behind the counter. The door he had noticed before was slightly ajar and revealed a soft yellow light from within. He pushed the door open to find an office with a small lamp atop a desk illuminating the wood paneled walls. Then he noticed an opened door in the back leading to another room. Maybe this was a way to a back door. He quickly stepped into the office. Glancing back at Uri, the Hungarian was still standing on the other side of the counter, pointy stick-head and all. Steven closed the door and locked it.

Chapter 13

Norman cleared his vision as he faded into his surroundings. He knew instinctively that he was in the parlor. Sitting on the floor with his knees up to his chest, Norman came to realize that he was staring down a gauntlet of sofas and chairs toward the stairway at the back of the parlor. He touched the cuts on his face.

Norman didn't usually think too much about his comings and goings but this time he was struck with a revelation. That glowing aura of a boy wasn't just his imagination nor was it a specter of some kind. It was real and it was hotly charged with the electricity of life. It had a vibrant, beating heart. And Norman… did not. The wound on his chest was deep. He put his thumb into it through the slit in his shirt and rotated it as he pushed down between his ribs. No pain. No warmth.

A loud thud on the floor startled Norman. He got up on his feet and looked around. He spotted the headless fat man down on his hands and knees near the front of the parlor. Norman stepped slowly toward the big, bloated body as it awkwardly tried to gain balance, getting on its feet using an end table for support. As Norman approached the staggering body, he noticed a split branch of wood sticking out of its neck stump.

He cautiously stepped back when the headless man began to move in his direction. Without a head it couldn't see, hear or smell but yet sensed Norman and started to walk toward him. Stepping aside a few steps, putting a sofa between himself and the body, Norman was amused when it stumbled and fell on the floor again.

There was a slight creaking sound behind Norman. He looked around but didn't see anything. Standing still he listened carefully. A repeating squeak of a floorboard was coming from underneath an end table. Norman crouched down to get a closer look. It was the man's head. It was facing upward, swaying back and forth from side to side. Norman was puzzled. Each time the head rolled back to its upward facing position, its jaw jutted in the opposite direction causing the head to roll, almost in the same way as a kid on a swing-set kicking backward and forward. The man's eyes shifted from side to side in sync with the jaw in an effort to increase the momentum. To Norman's amusement, the head rolled far enough to come to a rest on its left ear. It looked up at him with bland curiosity.

Norman reached under the table and picked it up by its white beard and held it upside down. Raising it to his eye level, the head looked at Norman and its eyes grew wide, incredulous. It mouthed something but there was no sound. Norman flipped the head over holding it upright by its hair. It again formed a word with its lips and tongue. And then it dawned on Norman who this was, and he recognized what it was mouthing: *"Minion."*

It was Uri.

Norman was immediately overwhelmed by the memory of the last time he had seen him. It was when Norman was in the basement, hanging by his left hand wedged in the clothes chute door on the ceiling above the washer and dryer. Uri had crashed into the door of the utility room and screamed in horror. He cried out, "My Minion. Oh, my poor Minion. Who has done dis to you? Why? My Minion. My Minion…" Norman remembered looking down at the sobbing Uri as he was struggling to take his last breath. He hung there wincing from his left hand being crushed in the chute door by his own weight, blood running down his face, and a weapon buried in his chest. His vision blurred from the blood oozing out from where his eyelids had been cut and ripped off. Norman's final memory was seeing the repeated reflection of his bloody eyes from the shiny pipes. Knowing it was his final breath, he held it as long as he could until he drifted away into the painlessness of death.

And now here he was, reunited with old Papa Bear Uri, his big round head framed by his white fluffy hair. With his free hand, Norman touched the cuts on his own face. Uri gave him a sullen, pouting expression apparently remembering that day as well.

Norman suddenly felt a big, meaty hand on his shoulder. He looked up to see Uri reaching out for his own head. Norman jerked the head away, pushed Uri's hand off his shoulder and slid away from the upright body. He quickly moved behind a sofa away from Uri's reach. Holding the head under his arm, Norman wagged his index finger at Uri's body. Then he thought better of it and wagged the finger at Uri's face instead.

Most of Norman's life had been under the control of Uri. And although Uri, or Papa Bear as he had called him, saved him from the streets and gave him a home, Norman was not about to pass up this opportunity to turn the tables. Norman liked the idea of being in control. He savored the feeling of empowerment. And there is no greater control one can have over an individual than when you have their head. Norman grinned. He knew exactly what he was going to do. He took the head under his arm and started towards the stairway. Uri's body clumsily followed.

Chapter 14

T he room behind the office was dark. Steven stepped in and patted the wall to his side for a light switch. Squinting, he could see a string hanging from the ceiling with a small object hanging at the end. This was either a spider or a string for a light. Stepping closer, Steven reached out and pulled on it. The room illuminated. It wasn't a blotchy yellow-brown light that was produced from the lamps in the parlor; nor was it the stark blue-white florescent light from the basement. The room was filled with a warm, even glow from a chandelier obtrusively hanging from the low ceiling. It had six bulbs shaped like flames. Steven almost had to duck to step beyond it.

This must be Uri's living quarters. It was a long narrow room extending toward the back of the building with a bed against the wall towards the far end. A small kitchenette on the opposite wall was complete with a counter, sink and microwave oven. There was a small dorm-sized refrigerator off to the side of the counter. The room was filled with the odor of bad cologne mixed with rotten bananas.

Steven went right for the refrigerator, his dehydration taking priority. He silently rejoiced to find three unopened bottles of Gatorade. He chugged one down in fifteen seconds spilling a quarter of it on his sweater. He was out of breath. He leaned against the counter, gasping for air.

After a moment of recuperation, Steven unscrewed the cap off the second bottle. Before drinking any, he turned on the cold water and leaned over the sink. As he splashed water on his face, he could see dirt and blood swirl down the drain. He splashed the water more aggressively and scrubbed his face with his hands. A small chunk of something fell from his hair and pinged against the faucet as it tumbled into the sink. Steven picked it up between his thumb and forefinger and looked closely at it while water ran off his face. It was part of a tooth. It must have been Uri's. Steven looked out into the office and assured himself the door to the parlor was still shut. He wiped his face with his sleeve not trusting the cleanliness of the towel hanging from a hook on the wall.

He felt safe here, for the moment at least. He knew, though, that he could not let his guard down and become passive. Not even for one second. He took a slug of Gatorade and began to look around the room for a weapon. What kind of anti-demon, anti-headless Hungarian defense mechanisms could he find?

Steven noticed an old-style phonograph with a crank and a cornucopia shaped sound horn. There were at least a few dozen albums on the shelf above the phonograph. Surely Uri didn't use this old phonograph, with its jagged metal needle, on these modern LP albums? The albums were probably ruined after the first time they were played.

At the end of the shelf there were some photographs. Three of the pictures were more prominent than the others, all having the same frames decorated with etched gold and black ivy. All three pictures appeared to be wedding photos of Uri and each of his brides. Steven vaguely recalled Uri blabbing on about his brothers and his wives.

The wedding picture on the far left showed Uri and a woman in a long, laced gown standing in front of a church. Uri wore a white tuxedo comically offset by his thick, black-rimmed glasses and black bow tie. His bride wore sunglasses and held a cane. She must have been blind. Both looked to be in their sixties; this must have been Uri's most recent wife.

The next picture was taken in front of the same church. This time Uri wore a black suit with a striped tie and looked quite a bit younger but no less overweight. His bride was short and chubby and was only as tall as Uri's shoulders. She held onto a bouquet of flowers and had a toothy smile. Her boyish Dutch-style haircut with curtain rod bangs seemed to accentuate her chubby, ruddy cheeks. Her eyes were small, black dots.

The third wedding picture was in black and white and was taken of Uri and his bride inside of a church at an altar. She was at least four inches taller than Uri. Long blond hair flowed out from her veil, which was pulled back away from her face. Steven glanced at some of the other pictures. There was Uri looking very young, possibly a teenager, grouped with two other young men. Maybe these were Uri's brothers. Even in his youth Uri had a big round belly. Apparently, he was fat his entire life. There was even a picture of Uri sitting in a jail cell. Precious moments in life.

He was drawn back to the photograph of Uri's first marriage. Something struck him about the bride. He looked closely at her face and sensed there was something familiar about her.

Steven heard a whisper directly behind his head, "Steeee-ven."

He quickly jerked around and put his hands up, ready to fight. The room was empty. This was the same voice he heard down in the basement coming from the room with the pipes. Then it occurred to him that he had heard this voice say his name before he had even come to the Inn. It was when he was having his meltdown in the cafeteria at work. That's right, Steven thought. He remembered hearing his name and how it seemed to cause his belligerent left side to cease attacking long enough for him to get up and run away.

It was his mother's voice and it had shrieked his name as clear as a bell.

Steven looked at the photo in amazement. It just couldn't be, but it was. It was Steven's mother. The smile gave it away. He had seen it a dozen times in old photo albums his grandmother kept. She had dark eyes that seemed to slant in a sad expression even though her mouth projected a bright, happy smile. Her high cheek bones and a somewhat pointy chin were unmistakable.

Steven stared at the picture. He had difficulty accepting the idea that his mother had been married to the man he apparently murdered with a shovel. He picked up the frame and turned it over. Frantically Steven ripped off the back support and pulled out the photograph. There was no date, or any other info written on the back. He turned it over and looked at it again. Did his mother live here once with Uri? Was this before or after he was born? Did Steven's father know about Uri or this place?

Steven had seen photos of his father but had no memories of him. In fact, he kept one picture of him on his apartment wall in the hallway. It was a picture of Steven as a toddler sitting on his father's lap wearing a railroad engineer's hat. His father had looked very much like Steven does now but with a stronger jaw and confidence in his eyes. It was his understanding that his father would spend up to eight months a year in Alaska on an offshore oil rig. Apparently, he died in an accident at the site when Steven was only two. A malfunctioning wench had launched a crowbar under his chin, up through his face and into his brain. Steven likened his windmill accident to his father's misfortune, the difference being that he was a survivor. In an unusual way the picture in Steven's Hall gave him encouragement.

Steven figured that his mother must have married Uri sometime after his father died. She didn't look young enough to have been married to him before his father. To his knowledge, she was committed to the psychiatric ward at the mental hospital when Steven was five so she must have had only a brief relationship with Uri. What in the world could she have possibly found appealing about that fat Hungarian?

"Steeeeeee-veeeeeeeen…"

Frozen in his steps, Steven looked around the room. He was still alone but felt a creeping cold wave move up his spine. "Oh my God," Steven said aloud. He could barely come to grips with the notion that his mother could actually still be alive somewhere in this freaky Inn. Maybe she needs help, he thought. But how could she know I'm here? Unless… unless she's become one of them. Maybe she was like that weird demon boy and the resurrected headless Uri. But what exactly were they? Steven didn't believe in ghosts. On the other hand, he didn't *disbelieve* in ghosts. He had seen plenty of spiritualists and ghost hunters on TV to know that many people did believe in them. Grandma certainly believed.

When Steven first noticed the demon child sitting on the stairs, it came and went in flashes. Similar to when he saw it again in the basement. It was no more than a fleeting apparition. But out in the parlor he *felt* it touch his eye and he also felt the force of his punch to its chest connect and send him flying. He felt Uri's tight grip on his ankles. Steven pulled up his pant leg and exposed a purple contusion where Uri had gripped him tightly. There was nothing unreal about it. But it was impossible.

Again, he heard his name in a hoarse whisper, "Steee-ven."

Standing perfectly still, Steven listened for the direction the voice might be coming from. After a moment he realized that he had been in Uri's room for a few minutes and there was no attempt by Uri or the demon child to get in the room. It was very quiet.

Steven grabbed the Gatorade bottle he had opened and started to walk back to the parlor door on the other side of the office. Leaving Uri's room, he considered turning the light off but decided he didn't want to hear his mother's voice hissing from the darkness. The only sound was the slight creak from the old wooden floor beneath his steps.

He cautiously stood by the closed door to the parlor and listened. There was nothing, it was calm. Steven slowly opened the door and peered out. No one was in sight. He opened the door enough to sidle out towards the check-in counter. The coast was clear. Steven stood still for a moment. Then he heard the voice again, "Stee-veeen." It was coming from the back of the parlor, maybe up the stairs. "Steven, heeeelp meeee." The decrepit cry gave Steven chills. As he began to make his way to the front door, Steven was aware of his loud footsteps as his shoes stuck to the drying blood on the floor. He needed to get out of this place.

Moving around the corner he was horrified to find Uri's body still planted against the door. Steven stopped in his tracks and stared. "What the hell?" He was dumbfounded and didn't know what to do. The headless corpse was laying there blocking his escape just as it had been when he first came back up to the parlor. But....

"Steeee-ven." The shriek was louder. It was definitely coming from up the stairs. Steven turned around and made a dash back into the office and closed the door behind him, took a deep breath and locked it. Gatorade still in hand, Steven went back to Uri's room and sat down on his bed. Once again he lifted his pant leg and examined the bruises. There is no way I could have imagined this, Steven thought. All that he went through back in the parlor couldn't have been his imagination. Steven sat there perplexed. He still felt an odd chill in his eye from the demon boy's bony finger.

It occurred to Steven that his annoying child self hadn't made its presence since he had felt it boil up causing him to strike out at the little demon. Steven began to sense the slightly distant sound of the stupid circus music beginning to build in his head. And then it abruptly went away. Okay, so the worm was present. It was just sitting in the background observing. Very nice to hear from you again, Steven said to himself sarcastically. Steven seemed to be getting used to the idea of sharing his head with it. Considering all the effort he had put into suppressing it throughout most of his life, this seemed to be the solution. Okay, not that it felt normal, but it was acceptable.

Steven already had conceded that it wasn't until he purposefully let the worm rise to meet him at his conscious level that he started to see the demon child. Maybe this horror show has all been a fabrication or an illusion generated by his lonely and possibly demented former child as way of lashing out at him. If it could control what he sees and feels, what better way for that little shit to get back at him for all those years of suppression? The music started again.

"Oh shut up!" Steven said. And the music stopped.

He again felt his ankles. After all he had been through, he was not about to easily concede that this was all in his mind, from his adult self or his child self. Steven pondered on this and took a gulp of the Gatorade. It's as though I'm living in two worlds, he wondered. And maybe that's it. Maybe the worm has sight into their world. But it wasn't just sight. There was more to it than that.

"Steeeeeeeee-veeen please..."

This time Steven felt his heart sink when he heard his mother calling his name. And he knew that lowly feeling was coming from his child self. Steven took another drink. This is just insane, he thought. But he couldn't help but be overwhelmed with the feeling that he wanted to be with his mother. He never really felt this way before, at least not since the windmill accident.

Steven allowed the child in him to weep. But only for a minute. He needed answers.

Chapter 15

Norman carried the head with both of his spindly arms down the hall of the second floor. The sound of the grinder grew louder. When he arrived at Mrs. Crawford's door, he stopped for a moment and let his eyes get accustomed to the bright light emanating from below the door. After a moment, the door opened slightly allowing the white light to bleed out into the hallway. Norman patiently waited until it had become tolerable enough for him to see again. He held Uri's head by the hair as he slowly pushed the door open. The door creaked loudly but did not disturb Mrs. Crawford as she continued her grinding.

Norman did not enter the room initially but instead held Uri's head across the threshold of the door, face first. He watched Uri's expression as his eyes grew large and mouth opened slightly. Uri silently said something. Norman rotated the head, so it was facing him. Uri

"

had a desperate look about him and was mouthing the word "No."

Using Uri's face, he pushed the door open wider and stepped in the room. Both Norman and Uri watched Mrs. Crawford as she wildly moved her body with large circular strokes hanging on to the grinder handle with both hands. As usual, there was nothing in the grinder. Norman moved into the room with the head and stood next to Mrs. Crawford. The door closed behind him.

He knew that she sensed him there. It never seemed to bother her that he would occasionally come to her room and sit and stare. Of the three oddball women at the Inn, Norman felt an unusual respect for Mrs. Crawford. She was the most recent to become a resident, at least until Uri popped up. He first saw her in this room doing exactly what she was doing now, grinding. Like the bag lady upstairs, Norman didn't know Mrs. Crawford. She couldn't talk but mostly would just cackle or cough and then gag. She always gagged from not being able to close her mouth. Norman didn't know anything about her other than she liked her grinder. He named her Mrs. Crawford just because it seemed to fit.

Norman reached over the grinder and set Uri's head on the counter laying it on its side. Uri stared upward at Mrs. Crawford with wide eyes as she continued her grinding uninterrupted. Norman watched with patience to see what would happen when Mrs. Crawford finally recognized Uri. But she was blind. She couldn't see that his head was sitting right in front of her just dying to be noticed.

The door crashed open and in came Uri's staggering body. It stood for a moment and then began to move toward Norman causing him to take a step back.

The door creaked as it slowly closed by itself.

As Uri's body waddled forward, it reached outward. It wanted its head. Norman looked over to Uri's head and noticed his eyes frantically darting back and forth from Mrs. Crawford to his body. Uri's headless torso stopped short of the counter and began to lean forward extending his arm over the grinder toward his head.

Norman watched carefully and waited for the right moment. And then he lunged forward grabbing Uri's wrist with both hands decisively shoving his hand down into the open feeder of the grinder. Mrs. Crawford was in her downward motion of the handle when Uri's fingers caught in the auger blades. His bones twisted and cracked. Mrs. Crawford let out a howl. The handle rose high as she faced upward toward the ceiling. And again, it came down with a forceful stroke sucking Uri's hand further down into the grinder. Now she chortled with hideous laughter, delighted to feel the reluctant bulk of bones and tissue being dismantled. She swung the handle back up to its apex.

Using his free hand, Uri stopped her downward motion with a firm grip on her forearm. Like wax figures, everyone stood perfectly still for a moment until Mrs. Crawford slowly turned her head in the direction of Uri's body. Although blind, she glared intently.

In a single motion, she slung her free arm backward, hand extended above her head. A large cleaver that hung on the wall suddenly zipped through the air, handle connecting to her hand as she swung forward with lightning speed. The sharp blade whisked through Uri's arm right at the elbow. Uri began wobbling on his feet. Still gripping Mrs. Crawford's forearm, Uri's arm dangled freely. Mrs. Crawford, still gazing at Uri's body, jerked the handle down swiftly generating a loud crunch as Uri's lower hand bones gnashed together in the grinder.

Uri began to thrash, yanking at his pulverized hand trying to free himself. He twisted and pulled, his hand not budging from the grinder. Mrs. Crawford lifted the cleaver high and swung it down once again with a whoosh. Uri's other arm was now also severed at the elbow, leaving him with two stumps. Uri's head, still resting on the counter, closed its eyes and forced them to stay shut. Uri's body took a tentative step toward Norman, paused and then reeled backward. The door swung open on its own with a crash. Reaching the doorway, Uri stumbled out into the hallway and fell hard making a thud on the floor that could even be felt by Uri's head on the counter. Mrs. Crawford cackled and gasped and then she gagged.

Norman was amused by Uri's predicament. His arms being mere stubs made it difficult for him to shift his weight from his bloated belly to his knees. He was like a turtle stranded on its back. Norman looked back to Mrs. Crawford who had continued grinding away at Uri's arm. He noticed the meat cleaver had been returned to the wall. He also saw that Mrs. Crawford had put Uri's other arm on the countertop, save for later.

Norman's attention went to the output of the grinder where flesh and pieces of bone were being forced out through the grinder's blade plate. Small chunks of loosely connected tissue were streaming down to the counter onto a growing pile of gore.

Norman adored Mrs. Crawford.

Chapter 16

The closest Steven was able to come to finding a weapon was a polka dot umbrella. In the kitchenette there were utensils including a four inch steak knife but somehow this didn't seem like much of a weapon considering how easily Uri ingested the shovel handle. Steven looked in the lower cupboards and behind furniture hoping to come across a baseball bat or maybe a golf club.

Getting on his hands and knees, he pulled the bedspread up from the floor and looked under the bed. Steven reached underneath and pulled out a tray.

"What have we here?"

The tin tray was probably an old TV tray without its legs. It was beige displaying a faded image of a cowboy on a bucking bronco. Steven scanned over the objects dispersed on the tray: wads of foil, two blackened spoons, miniature oil lamp, matches and a lighter, six narrow syringes, rubber tube and a number of small, envelop shaped packages.

Uri was a junkie.

Steven pushed the tray back under the bed. He got off the floor and glanced around the room again, giving the umbrella a brief second look. He looked back at the photographs on the shelf and wondered about Uri's time in jail. Maybe he got caught dealing heroine out of the Inn. It wouldn't be a big surprise if Uri and his brothers had a little smuggling business using their Hungarian connections. Steven again looked at the picture of his mother and Uri at the altar. Was his mother a junkie too?

Steven walked out of the back room and into the office continuing his search, looking around the desk. He opened the upper drawers to find a lot of emptiness other than a few receipts, pens and pencils. However, the larger bottom drawer was filled with all kinds of junk like rulers, staplers, light bulbs and scissors. Among the miscellaneous was a large flashlight. Steven picked it up and felt the heft of four size 'D' batteries. It emanated a bright beam upon flicking the switch. Steven turned it off. He wasn't quite sure what he was in store for, but he didn't want to bring attention to himself unnecessarily by waving around a small search light.

"Steeeeeeee-veeeeeen."

The icy whisper of the voice raised the hair on Steven's arms. His mother was calling for him. He felt the childish pain of heartache rise inside of him, but he squelched it. He couldn't give in to feelings of insecurity and loneliness; he had to be smart. He had to be in control. There was no room for bad judgment from an emotional crisis. If he was going to look for his mother in this hotel from hell he would have to be steady and determined.

Steven knew he had nothing to lose. He felt like he was here for a reason. All of this coming down on him at once, the meltdown at work, killing Uri, fending off ghosts, or whatever they were. It all started happening after he first laid eyes on this creepy building. And that was about the time he started hearing his mother calling him. He had to find her. And if he confronted the headless Hungarian, it would be wiser to just avoid him rather than engage in a fight. Steven already knew he could get physical with Norman if necessary.

"Norman? Where the hell did that come from?" Steven surprised himself, the name just popping out of his head. "How did I know that?" he said aloud alone in the office. Norman. Not only was it a fitting name, but it was also familiar. *Norman.*

Steven stood for a moment, paying attention to the worm, which he sensed was present but quiet. He waited for an inkling of an indication that it knew something about that boy with the wide eyes and the cuts on his face. Norman. How did he know his name was Norman? Apparently, no insight was forthcoming. He looked back to the warm chandelier light emanating from the back room. Carrying the flashlight, Steven returned to the room and went to the pictures on the shelf. Not more than a dozen pictures in all. He briefly scanned through each of them but no trace of a scrawny little kid. You'd think if Uri had any children, he would have kept at least one picture.

Distant creaking and bumping sounds could be heard from somewhere in the Inn. Steven looked back to the picture of his mom one last time. His only memories of her were from brief flashbacks from before his accident but they were brief and fragmented at best. Those fleeting thoughts were always accompanied by an uncomfortably lowly feeling. Was there never any joy in his relationship with his mother? Had she been too mentally disturbed to love her only son? Steven felt a sense of resentment and anger. He wisely used these feelings to build up his courage.

He turned and purposefully walked out of the room back into the office. He slowly approached the door to the parlor taking small, quick steps. Opening the door slightly, he peered out. Scanning from the front door to the back stairway, the parlor was empty. Steven opened the door all the way and stepped out. Refusing to look toward the corpse at the front door, Steven turned to his right and walked directly toward the stairway, retracing his steps from when he had earlier entered the parlor from the basement. He had almost forgotten about the pool of blood on the floor until his shoes began making loud sticky sounds as he walked.

Stopping about halfway to the stairs, Steven stood still and listened. It was quiet again except for a faint scratching sound, maybe it was rainfall hitting the roof or wind blowing a tree against a window. He slowly walked to the stairs holding the unlit flashlight up to his chest with both hands. As he approached the stairs he looked down and noticed his bloody footprints leaving the parlor toward the basement. It was still perplexing how he could have flipped out and hacked away at Uri with a shovel. Steven looked down at the cold cement stairs that lead to the dreary basement thinking about seeing all those eyes staring at him reflecting from the menagerie of pipes. He stepped back and moved toward the stairs leading up to the next floor.

He noticed the wood stairs were covered with a thick layer of dust. Steven put his right foot on the first step then removed it. An obvious footprint was made in the dust. Looking up toward the next landing, it was apparent that these steps had not been used in a very long time. Didn't Uri ever clean or do any maintenance on the rooms upstairs? Then he remembered Uri saying this place was condemned. Steven realized that he'd better watch his step.

He put his left hand on the railing but removed it once he saw that it was also covered with dust. He put a tentative foot on the first step. One foot after the other, he slowly moved up the stairs. It wasn't until he reached the landing halfway to the second floor that he became aware of how hard his heart was beating. He stopped for a moment and tried to calm down a little. Taking a deep breath, he felt a bead of sweat roll down the side of his face. He briefly thought about his Land Rover parked outside. He wanted to leave. "Do this," Steven said quietly through clenched teeth. He cautiously went up the stairs.

He looked upward and saw cobwebs hanging from every corner. It was dark although he could vaguely sense a dim light coming from somewhere on the second floor. As he ascended slowly up the stairs, he felt it getting noticeably colder. He stopped about five steps from the top and listened. Again, he heard the scratching sound. It was steady. It was louder now and no longer sounded like rain. His heart started to race again when he made out the faint sound of sobbing. Not knowing where it was coming from, Steven looked back down the stairs at the yellowish-brown glow from the parlor lamps. He thought about the warm light from the chandelier back in the safety of Uri's room and realized how far away it seemed.

Looking back up, Steven quietly began to move up the stairs. As his eyes reached the level of the second floor, he peered down the hallway looking for any signs of movement. It was very dim, almost hazy. He could see a hanging light bulb about halfway down the hall. It was illuminated emitting only a soft, grayish glow. It was just enough light to see the silhouettes of the cobwebs hanging from the ceiling and draping the walls. It felt even colder. Steven got the chills. He took another step, his head and shoulders now crossing the threshold of the second floor. Steven heard the scratching sound a little more clearly now. It came from somewhere down the hall accompanied by a slight echo from the emptiness of the building. Steven had to force his reluctant knee to rise to take another step up the stairs. He was shaking. As he slowly stepped up and onto the second floor, he continued to stare down the hallway looking for any movement. He stood and listened. The scratching sound stopped. Now it was apparent that the faint sobbing was coming from the next floor up. Steven looked at the next flight of steps. They were as dusty and dreary as the steps he had just ascended.

Suddenly the silence was broken by faint thuds coming from down the hallway. Squinting, Steven could see a strip of light emanating at the far end. Bam! The door at the end of the hall crashed open and someone was rushing out of the room. It was Uri, and he still had the shovel handle sticking out of his neck. His round bloated body fell hard to the hallway floor making another loud thud that shook the floor all the way down to where Steven stood. Without hesitation he took quick steps up the stairs toward the third floor, only briefly looking back to see Uri squirming on the floor at the end of the hallway. Steven was horrified to see that Uri no longer had any arms, only flailing stubs.

Steven moved swiftly up the stairs on his tip toes, consciously raising his knees high to avoid stumbling. Moving past the mid-floor landing, the air grew colder and darker. There didn't appear to be any light coming from the third floor. He wanted to turn on the flashlight but thought better of it and opened his eyes as wide as possible trying to acclimate to the darkness. The next thing he knew, Steven found himself with a face full of cobwebs. He paused on the stairs to clear his eyes and mouth.

"Steeeee-veeeen." The hissing voice was coming from somewhere on the third floor.

Looking over the top step, he peered down the hallway. He could barely make out the doors to the first few rooms but beyond that the hall was too dark to see anything. Steven attempted to quietly say "mom", but nothing came out. His sweaty face felt the sting of a chilly draft moving down the stairway.

Steven listened. The sobbing had stopped. He again heard the scratching, grinding sound from somewhere down on the second floor. Before moving up the stairs he glanced behind him making sure he wasn't being followed. Steven climbed slowly to the third floor. He stood still at the top of the stairs fully aware of the pace and strength of his heartbeat. The flashlight was shaking in his right hand. Looking down the hall, he still could not make out anything past the halfway point. Steven almost surprised himself when he flicked on the flashlight. The beam of light unsteadily shone down the hall revealing a mass of webs and dust. He noticed the vapors from his own breath floating into the beam of light. Quickly, Steven turned off the light and held his breath, carefully listening to see if he had unsettled anyone or anything from the bright light. Steven thought he heard breathing but couldn't really tell. He paused for a moment trying to figure out what to do next. The longer he stood there at the top of the stairs, the more his knees began to wobble. Steven had to make a decision. He knew he either needed to flee right now and hopefully get out of the building alive or he needed to continue to find his mother. He had come this far. Steven forced himself to take one reluctant step down the hall. The floor responded with a creak as he took another shaky step forward.

Steven crept down the hall holding the unlit flashlight ahead of his face to intercept the cobwebs. With each footstep the old floor squeaked. He listened for the sobbing or any movement but heard nothing. After about ten steps down the hall, he stopped at the first door on his left. He looked down and could see a faint glow coming from under the door. Steven stood and listened. After a few seconds he slowly turned the handle. But before he opened the door, he held the flashlight above his head ready to strike at… well, whatever may be waiting on the other side.

The door opened without a sound, stretching cobwebs from the door jamb into the room. There was a window in the room partially covered with a tattered shade. The faint glow in the room was coming from the ambient outside light creeping in through the torn window shade. There was barely enough light to see that the room was filled with dust and cobwebs just like the hallway. As Steven stepped into the doorway, pushing webs aside with the flashlight, he could see the room was decorated with shelves and shelves of dolls. Various sized dolls all gray and mottled in appearance from years of dust buildup. The room had a sharp vinegary odor.

Steven was satisfied that he was alone in the room. He wanted to turn on the flashlight and get a better look. He stuck his head out into the hall and looked both ways. He was still alone. He stepped back in the room, quietly closed the door and switched on the flashlight.

It was amazing. Three of the four walls in the room each had three shelves, all fully populated with dolls. Cobwebs strung across the rows and veiled their round porcelain faces. Steven shone the light slowly across the display. Even though the dolls were filthy, he noticed that each of them had its eyes shut. Not one doll had its eyes in the open position.

There was a bare mattress lying on the floor in the corner of the room. Steven could see an old-style sewing machine against the far wall. Next to it were stacks of cloth and a basket full of miscellaneous sewing items such as buttons, scissors, knitting needles, etc. On the other side of the sewing machine were more piles of clothes, an old burlap sack, cardboard boxes and other junk. There was also a table against the wall near the door that provided ample space for one small item, a narrow vase propping up a single dried-up rose. It was perfectly placed in the absolute center of the table. Like all the other objects in the room, it was covered with years of airborne sediment giving the mauve flower a dirty yet almost dewy texture. Steven blew a puff of air at the crispy rose. A plume of dust scattered off into the room.

Steven heard something move. He stood motionless. He pointed the flashlight to a narrow door at the back of the room, presumably a bathroom. Once again, he heard his heart pounding. He slowly walked toward the bathroom door clearing away cobwebs as they were encountered. When he reached the bathroom door, he subconsciously told himself to open it without giving himself a chance to build up too much fear. Without hesitation he jerked the door open and quickly scanned the room with his flashlight. The small bathroom had been gutted. There was no shower and no toilet. Only bare plumbing could be found protruding from the floor and the wall. Again, he heard a rustling noise but this time it was coming from behind him in the room. Someone's coming, he thought. Steven quickly turned off the flashlight and stepped into the bathroom. He closed the door all but an inch and stood perfectly still, peering out into the room.

The burlap sack moved. There was something inside of it. Steven felt his heart crawl up into his throat. He continued to remain motionless although he felt his left leg weaken from his shaking knee. He stiffened both of his legs and made himself sturdy. He held his breath as he carefully watched the burlap sack move again in the dimly lit room. Then abruptly it fell away from the wall with a dull thud on the floor. Steven held the flashlight firm in his left hand while holding his mouth with the other, trying to keep from accidentally making a sound. Bulges and lumps protruded from the formless blob in the bag. It remained closed cinched with a thick rope.

Then Steven heard a mewing sound, but not quite like a cat. It had an almost humming lilt to it. The burlap sack began to rock back and forth. It then became apparent that the rhythm behind the humming was synchronized with the rocking. There was someone inside the sack. Steven let out his breath and felt his whole body slacken with the exhale.

The humming abruptly stopped.

"Steeeee-ven." The dry cry of his name could be heard from somewhere out in the hall.

"Laaaa-laa" mimicked the voice from within the bag.

After a moment, the childish sound of soft humming from the bag returned. Steven leaned against the wall inside the bathroom to steady himself. As he watched the burlap sack sway back and forth, he was dumbfounded. After a moment he knew he needed to get out of this eerie doll room. But before he could act, he noticed the door to the hallway was slowly opening. Steven moved back slightly and closed the bathroom door all but just a sliver, just enough to look out across the room toward the hallway door.

It was Norman, the demon boy. He stood in the doorway with a freakish grin. He held something large under one of his arms and cupped something in the palm of his other hand. It was too dark for Steven to make out what he had.

The soft humming was becoming agitated, almost whiny. Steven noticed the burlap sack was no longer rocking but instead seemed to be jerking as though whatever was in it wanted to get out. Norman stepping into the room and slowly approached the bag. Now the whiny humming began begging, "Pleeeease. Please feeeeeed meeeeeee."

He felt a familiar chill zip up his spine. It was all Steven could do to stand perfectly still. He watched intently through the crack in the door. He watched Norman emerge into the faint glow in the center of the room revealing the furry white object under his arm. As he was putting it on the floor, Steven was shocked to discover it was a head. It was Uri's head. Norman had Uri's head and he was setting it down on the floor next to the burlap sack. As he laid the head down on its ear, Steven saw with horror the eyes of the head move back and forth. And then all at once, Uri looked directly at Steven's eyes. He had somehow spotted him peering out from the bathroom. Again, Steven had to force himself to steady his legs and keep his balance. A fresh bead of sweat rolled down his left temple.

"I'm sooo hungry…" cried from the bag.

Steven still couldn't make out what Norman was holding in his extended hand. The little demon knelt next to the burlap sack and with his free hand unraveled the rope. The opened end of the sack fell gently on the floor next to Uri's head.

"Oh please, I'm just soooo hungry." The pitch of the voice went from being high and whiny down to a low tone. It was a woman's voice.

Steven noticed Uri's attention was now focused on the opening of the sack. Slowly, something was squirming out.

Norman turned his hand over and dumped a wad of gooey substance on the floor. Plop.

The sack had fallen back exposing a woman's head and shoulders. She was grayish green. Her eyes were big dark purple circles. Steven looked closely and in horror saw that her eyes were permanently closed. Each eyelid was fastened shut by small safety pins. Below the safety pin under the left eye was a quarter-sized pink button, apparently sewn onto her cheek. Under the corner of her right eye were a series of smaller buttons streaming down to her cheek in an obvious attempt to emulate tears. Steven had never dreamt such a nightmare could exist.

Wide eyed, Uri pushed his jaw against the floor to get a better angle.

"… A little bit of fooood. Pleeease?"

Norman stood erect. A big grin emerged.

Slam! As if suddenly aware of the treasured substance Norman dumped in front of her, the lady smashed her button laced face down upon it, crashing hard against the wood floor. She let out a deep, raspy growl like an old lion. Steven winced. Then he heard a snorting, sucking sound followed by a big gulp. As fast as this assault on the goop had started, it was over. The room was again silent. Steven covered his mouth.

The little woman with the round face, who looked to be a victim of a very cruel and severe torture, turned out to be a beast. Steven could see globs of the weird substance oozing off the side of her mouth as she turned her head upward toward Norman. Then, in a very tiny girly voice, "More please."

Norman continued to look down at her in a daze. His evil grin and overly wide eyes revealed his insane nature. He continued to stare, as though hypnotized. And then Steven almost couldn't believe his eyes. Norman began to fade away. He could barely see right through him until a moment later he was completely gone. Steven blinked a few times. Norman was no longer there.

Steven stood still. He didn't know what to make of all this. He couldn't think. He looked down and saw that Uri was glancing back and forth between him and the woman in the sack.

"I WANT MORE!!" She belted out with a roar. Steven took a step back. Uri closed his eyes tightly. The woman's body twisted from inside the bag.

To Steven's astonishment, Norman was back in the room, standing right where he had been before. He slumped over and picked up Uri's head off the floor by his hair. In one motion, he reached with the other hand and grabbed the opened end of the burlap sack and pulled it back. Then he took Uri's head and shoved it inside. Immediately the freakish woman retreated down into the bag. Norman picked up the rope off the floor and slowly began to wind it around the opening, cinching it shut. Then he let it go and took a step back. A few bulges could be seen moving from within the sack. Steven, feeling weak in the knees, began to crouch down.

The woman let out a long, ear-piercing scream. This was followed by a moment of silence. And then the feeding frenzy commenced. Snorting, growling, crunching, ripping, gulping... The bag was tossing violently on the floor. Norman was grinning again, clapping his hands in glee. One of his hands seemed to be deformed.

Steven slid down on his butt. He peered out the crack to see if Norman had noticed him. The insane boy with the cuts on his face and the demonic grin just stood there, staring down at the flopping burlap sack. Steven closed his eyes and took a deep breath. If there was ever a time he was going to lose his mind and start screaming, this would be it. Instead, he kept his eyes closed and covered his ears yet he was unable to block out the crunching and gnawing.

A few moments had passed; the feasting noises had subsided. The woman in the bag was humming now. Apparently she was satisfied for the time being. Steven opened his eyes and peered out into the room. Other than the dolls lined up on the walls and the bulky burlap sack rocking on the floor, the room was empty. Norman was gone.

Chapter 17

The cold air wafted over Steven. He wallowed in the numbing bliss from the slight sting he felt on his sweaty face. He let himself escape for a moment as he sat in the dark bathroom.

He thought of the unsettling occasions in his adult life when he had flashbacks of his mother. He remembered seeing her long flowing hair spreading outward as she spun herself in a graceful response to the slow but passionate piano music. How much of this did Steven fabricate out of his own imagination? Was he simply filling in the gaps of his memory with idealistic, angelic visions of his mother? Why did he always feel pity afterwards? Steven could almost hear the distant metallic sound of the piano keys echoing the creepy melody.

Smack! Steven was suddenly slapped in the face. He opened his eyes as wide as possible but could see nothing. Smack! This time he received a lighter slap to his forehead.

Steven went cross-eyed trying to focus his eyes in the darkness as he became aware of the palm-facing hand a couple of inches in front of his face. He held his breath. A few seconds had passed and then the hand began to slowly move away. With an unexpected feeling of shame, Steven realized it was his own left hand that had slapped him. The sour memory of his meltdown in the cafeteria at work seeped up like heartburn.

That destructive monster in his head was the bane of his existence. It really didn't matter how the problem was approached, whether it was using exhaustive mental exercises or passively allowing it its own share of mind and mentality, it had a will of its own and it was going to strike when it wanted its way. It was going to blast load music like a screaming little sissy throwing a tantrum whenever it couldn't face reality. But no matter how childish it behaved, it was its own person and that made it difficult for Steven to accept even after all of these years. Thinking back to when he picked up the shovel in the parlor, Steven acknowledged the savage, killer qualities it possessed. This discovery was more than just a little disturbing. It was flat out chilling to know that the worm in his head was evil.

Steven let out a sigh and adhered to his own slap-in-the-face wakeup call and started to get back on his feet. He felt around the floor for the flashlight while he peered out into the room from the slightly cracked open door. The burlap sack had somehow rolled back to the wall and again was upright. It stood still and the humming had ceased. The room was empty.

He felt the weight of the flashlight in his left hand although he wasn't aware of picking it up. The thought of the worm being in control of a weapon worried Steven. Should he snatch it away with his right hand? That might be too confrontational and might kick off another violent episode. Then Steven wondered if his thoughts about this situation were being perceived. Had he lost all privacy to his alter identity? He sighed again, knowing what a basket case he had become.

Steven slowly opened the bathroom door. It made a creaking sound, so he jerked it open quickly. He stood there looking into the room with the dozens, if not hundreds of dusty dolls. Looking to the middle of the floor, Steven expected to see a small stain from where Norman dropped the gooey stuff for the bag lady to eat. There was nothing there but dust. Upon closer inspection, he could see his own footprints leading to the closet but nothing else. Why wasn't the floor marked up from the burlap sack flopping around? And what about Norman's footprints or a face print from Uri's head?

The slight feeling of vertigo caused Steven to swoon. The uncertainty of what was real and what was in his head, or the other part of his head, was overwhelming. He knew that he didn't imagine what had happened here yet there was no trace of any of it, other than the fear and nausea he was still recovering from.

He cautiously stepped out into the room. He considered turning on the flashlight, but it wasn't necessary as his eyes acclimated to the dim glow from the light emanating from the holes in the window shade. Steven kept his eyes on the burlap sack as he walked toward the hallway door. As he passed the bag he thought he saw it move. He stopped. After a moment he assured himself that the button faced nightmare in the bag didn't really exist. He turned away and started walking toward the door.

The bag fell on the floor behind him with a thud. Steven stiffened up. Looking over his shoulder he noticed a few bulges in the bag slowly moving. He turned back to the door and swallowed with difficulty. After taking one step he was stopped in his tracks from the chilling falsetto voice from behind him, "I'm sooooo huuuung-gry."

Steven had to get out, especially if this was a sign of a repeat visit from Norman. Not wanting to look back, he advanced toward the door.

Crack… Chomp, chomp. Apparently, there was still some of Uri's head left over in the bag.

Pulling the door open, Steven cautiously moved the webbing away and looked out into the hallway. Squinting, he could not make out anything in either direction. He had almost forgotten how much darker it was out in the hall than in the room. The ongoing sound of crunching from the burlap sack sounded like a dog gnawing on a rib-eye bone. Steven shuddered. Then he stepped out into the hallway and quietly closed the door behind him.

He was tempted to turn on his flashlight but was too afraid of what might be lurking about. Keeping his back to the wall, Steven sidled along making small steps while moving his head back and forth, looking up and down the hall for any sign of movement. He stopped about two steps from the door to the next room down and listened. He realized his back was covered in cobwebs and filth. As his eyes adjusted to the dark, he could see that the door to the room across the hall was open. It was very dark inside behind a doorway veiled with webbing. Steven held the unlit flashlight in front of him and moved slowly across the hall. As he brushed aside the curtain of webs, he could vaguely see into the room just enough to see that it was empty. Stepping inside the room it was evident that it was void of anything. No shelves, furniture or even a window. The featureless room was a cinder block dungeon.

Steven walked toward the center of the room. He became aware that his left hand was raising the flashlight. Without hesitation, he quickly reached over with his right hand and grabbed the flashlight, not wanting to light up the room and draw attention. To his surprise there was no response, no slapping or hitting or any other kind of retaliation. Steven didn't know what to make of this. Either the worm agreed that the flashlight should be left off or maybe it was showing some deference to his authority. Regardless, there seemed to be some level of compliance from his child-side and that was about the best that could be hoped for considering the circumstances.

There was something intriguing about this abysmal room. It was almost as though it was drawing him in like gravity. Feeling the rush of claustrophobia coming on, he did an about face. He plotted his steps back to the hallway before something unthinkable should happen, such as the door slamming shut, forever locking him in this pit.

Norman walked past the door.

Steven stood perfectly still holding his breath. After a few seconds he heard a door click open in the hallway. Norman must be going into the next room over. Then he heard a shrieking scream come from inside the room. Steven's spine chilled. He knew it was his mother.

"No! No! Noooooooo!! Get away from me you little shit!" The woman's shrill voice was intense. She sobbed and wailed in terror as she was being tormented. Steven's instinct was to run as fast as he could in the opposite direction but after a few moments the moaning suddenly just stopped. He stood with his feet locked to the floor and listened carefully. He thought he heard the clanging of something metallic before the woman gave way to a sorrowful moan, a long low groaning moan. This was followed by coughing and rasping. His mother was struggling, she was in pain. What the hell did Norman do to her?

Steven tried to move without having to talk himself through his fear. His legs reluctantly moved him toward the hall. The moaning reverted into sobbing, crying. As he reached the threshold of the hallway, he noticed the door to the room across the hall was also left open.

It was dark in there, probably another jail cell like this room. Steven glanced to his right and could see that a dingy bluish light was emanating from the room next to him. That must be his mother's room. Not seeing any sign of Norman, he dashed across the hall on his tip toes and into the dark room pushing aside cobwebs as he entered. Quickly, he moved inside the room putting his back flush against the wall. Just as he had expected, this room was also completely bare. The only difference was that this room had a single window that had been boarded up from the inside. It was cold and dank and smelled of rotting meat.

Steven carefully looked out across the hallway and down to the room where he could plainly hear his mother sobbing. Although he could see a bluish light from the room spilling out into the hall, there were no shadows, no sign of movement from within. He turned back to the dank room and took a deep breath. His mouth was dry. His palms were sweaty. He held the flashlight with a tight grip in his right hand. Steven was still determined about seeing this through. If that really was his mother in that room, then he had to finish this. He had to see her in her own flesh.

Slowly Steven walked out of the room into the hall. Again, he sidled along the wall looking intently toward the room emitting the blue murky light. After a few steps he could make out the foot of a bed. Atop the bed were two bare feet with long bony toes. Steven became aware of his teeth chattering and bit down hard clenching his jaw. He paused for a second before making another move. He lifted the flashlight high above his head ready to strike in case Norman was to exit into the hallway. As he stepped further down the hall, he could see that the bed in the room was a sort of a hospital bed with wheels and rails along the side of the mattress. The bare feet were bound to the bed rails by two-inch-thick straps at the ankles. He could see that the woman on the bed was wearing a white hospital gown covering her knees but exposing pale and bony shins covered with bruises. He briefly turned away and closed his eyes. He was not ready for this. But then again, would he ever be?

Steven took one step further and stopped when he could see Norman's back. He was in the room standing next to the bed looking down over his mother. Steven felt the heaviness of the flashlight. He could sneak up behind Norman and smash him over the head. Yes, the notion of taking out that little bastard demon child was very appealing. Steven's heart began to race. He sensed that familiar acidic taste of old nails. It was the taste of hatred. And he knew exactly where this was coming from. The worm was filled with burning hate and anger. Obviously, it somehow knew Norman and wanted nothing more than to destroy him.

Steven trustingly put the flashlight back in his left hand. He found himself in motion moving toward the room targeting Norman. As he approached the doorway, he raised the unlit flashlight over his head. But without warning Norman disappeared. One moment he was standing there and then the next moment he just fizzled out. Steven stood in the hall, frozen. The sobbing had stopped. The air was cold and still.

Looking into the room he could partially see the body of the woman on the bed from the chest down. Her spindly arms and bony hands were speckled with marks and bruises. Her nails were yellow and elongated, the surrounding skin receding around her thin fingers. Both of her arms were strapped to the bed rail. Dark purple rings around her wrists could be seen on her skin near the straps. She lay on top of the bed, her night clothes draping her frail, skeletal body. There was no sign of breathing. Her cavernous rib cage was perfectly still.

Steven held his breath watching for any sign of movement. He glanced down the hallway. It was completely dark. Cautiously he took two steps closer to the opened door but did not allow himself visibility to the face of the woman lying on the bed. He wasn't brave enough. The dingy blue light emanating from the room was not especially bright, but it irritated Steven's eyes. He squinted. Unlike the other rooms in this decrepit building, there was a slight sheen from the clean, beige tiled floor and the walls were painted a light shade of green. Steven noticed that the walls had a smooth contour instead of the stark cinder blocks he had come to expect. The sole window in the room was covered by long orange curtains. There was a faint buzzing sound coming from somewhere in the room. Or maybe it was in his head.

He gathered his courage. After taking a deep breath, he boldly stepped inside closing his eyes as he crossed the threshold. He stood for a moment, not quite willing to face the inevitable encounter with his mother. He was a mere three or four feet from the bed. Had he been noticed? Reluctantly Steven looked down to the floor as he opened his eyes. Lacking the courage to look up, he slowly walked to his left towards the foot of the bed. He noticed that his breath was visible. Apparently, he had unconsciously ignored the freezing temperature. The room was filled with the sterile smell of alcohol. Steven couldn't help but think he was standing in a hospital room although the air was thick and hazy from the cold dampness like a mausoleum.

Still looking toward the floor, he noticed something near the wall past the window. It was a pile of plastic syringes. The pile had to be over three feet high. There must have been well over a thousand of them. They all appeared clean, some with needles but most without. Almost automatically Steven shifted his focus to the bed. He peered at the woman's right arm and saw that her upward facing hand was so emaciated it didn't appear that any flesh separated her skin from her skeletal palm and digits. Then he noticed the odd clump of matter on her forearm. Bending forward to get a closer look, Steven was shocked to realize the clump was made up of broken needles. They were clustered over her inner elbow and branched down her arm along vein lines. Steven followed the broken needles up her arm toward her throat. Unable to take a breath he paused and then he looked directly at her face. His eyes grew twice their size.

She was dead. She was stone cold dead and gone. Her skin was ashen gray and was deeply wrinkled like a prune. Her wispy blond hair was matted on the left side of her head and was splayed out on the pillow to her right. Steven could see her scalp through her thin bangs. Both of her lips were stretched up and outward and were cracked from dehydration revealing wolfish yellow-brown teeth grotesquely protruding from receded gums.

Steven initially glanced around her face, past her eyes. He knew what was there but didn't want to face it. He shook his head. After a few moments he was finally able to take a deep breath and deliberately looked at her. Her eyes were closed. Atop both eyelids were two dull pennies, head side up. Gazing at the corpse, Steven attempted to connect the images from the memories of his mother, along with the wedding photo in Uri's room, to this decomposing body. It was his mother all right. It had to be. But Steven felt nothing. No remorse. No pity. No love.

He walked alongside the bed. The stench of death was apparent and almost made him want to vomit. He looked closer at all of the needles protruding from her arm. There were even more needles along her inner legs and ankles. There was even a small cluster on the sole of her right foot. Glancing back at the pile of syringes, Steven could not fathom what had happened to her. Or more like, what *was* happening to her. What was Norman doing to her? Steven felt a chill thinking about the screaming he heard coming from this room when

Norman was in there. Quickly he looked up at her face thinking he saw movement. But she was completely still, lying there like a mummy.

It was hard for him to look away from his mother's face and her raw expression of death. From his periphery vision at the foot of the bed, he could see the pennies placed on her eyes, and it gave the ghastly illusion that they were wide open, staring upward. The pennies gave him the creeps. The pennies, perfectly placed on the center of her eyelids, apparently were intended to keep her eyes closed during the rigor of the first hours of death. They were hideous. And he couldn't take his eyes off them.

Without looking away from his mother's pruned gray face, Steven stepped around to the side of the bed and slowly walked along her right side. His shoes scuffed slightly against the tile. Stopping a few feet short of the corpse's face, Steven held his elbows and looked down on his mother's body. The skeletal structure was so decrepit it seemed she would turn to dust upon touching her. Steven evaluated the clumps of needles on her long neck and limbs but had become unnerved by the pennies and returned his focus back to her face. His gaze was not reciprocating. In a moment of bravery, Steven reached out to remove those horrid pennies from her eyes. But as his hand approached her face, he started to shake and lost his nerve.

Steven said softly, "What happened to you, mother?" He felt hollow. Emotionally empty.

After a quiet moment in the morgue-like atmosphere, he thought he heard music in the distance. Then he realized where it was coming from. It was coming from within his head. Steven recalled how the crappy circus music blared in his mind when he first confronted Uri's mutilated body. It was the worm, and it was coming around. It occurred to Steven that it had not been present since he had encountered his mother. This was a surprise since it was why he had welled up with emotion back in Uri's room when he considered his mother may still be alive in this crazy place.

As Steven stared at the pennies, the music grew louder. This was disconcerting. If the worm was forcing the music, then it must be hiding from something. Hiding from what? Steven's head started pounding. The noise was building, and it was causing him pain. "Stop it." He said quietly through clinched teeth. He closed his eyes, grimacing, and put his fists up to his temples. "Stop it, God damn it!"

And the music stopped.

Steven slowly opened his eyes. He looked at his mother's face and noticed her mouth was closed. Steven's eyes opened wide as he felt his heart begin to pick up speed. The cracked and dehydrated lips that were curled back were now tightly pressed together. The strain on the skin caused deep lines extending from her mouth up her cheeks and down her chin and throat. She remained perfectly still, frozen in death. Steven looked down at her face and saw what could have been a slight movement of her chin, a slight quiver maybe. He cautiously leaned forward.

With an explosive force, his mother suddenly jerked against the constraints on her wrists forcing her chest upward and throwing her head backwards, her mouth gaping wide as she screamed. "Steeeeeeeeeee-veeeeeeen!!"

Steven was petrified, his blood instantly turning to ice. He tried to inhale but his throat was locked shut. His mother's thrashing was causing the bed to violently shake. He tried to step away, but his feet were stuck to the floor and his hands were tightly coupled to the bed rails. His body was so tense and rigid it caused a sharp pain to shoot up his back and neck. No matter how desperately he tried, he could not even look away. But somehow, a tiny squeak of a voice come from his mouth, "mom?"

"Steeee-eeee-ven!" hissed his mother.

"Mom? Mommy?"

Steven was not trying to speak. In fact, he was absolutely powerless in trying to move let alone make words. All he could do was stand there and stare as the rotting corpse of his mother convulsed and screamed, "Steeee-ven. Ste-eeeeee-ven. Steeeeeeeeeee-veeeeeeen!!"

He struggled to inhale. He was panicking and thought he might pass out. He wanted to close his eyes and make this nightmare go away. But he was a prisoner. He had absolutely no control over his body and was forced to confront this horror show. His mother's corpse continued jerking and thrashing violently. Her gown loosely hanging over her fleshless body exposed a sharp, bony pelvis. There were more clusters of broken needles on the sides and back of her neck. Her wispy hair flailed about. The stench of rotting death was overwhelming.

"Steeee-ven. Steven? Why, Steven? Whyyyyyyy?" the raspy voice cried.

Steven began shaking. His teeth were chattering uncontrollably. Again, he tried to move, to step backwards, but he was powerless.

"Steven. Steven. Why, Steven, did you put me in hell?" his mother hollered as she sobbed. After a moment she settled down a little but continued to toss her head from side to side. She grotesquely struggled to form words with her dry and decomposing lips. Amazingly, the pennies continued to be stuck to her eyelids. Thank God she couldn't open her eyes, Steven thought.

He looked into her gaping mouth as she yowled. Her tongue was gray and shriveled causing Steven to get weak in his knees. Suddenly he felt the hot bile from his stomach emerge in his mouth. He was going to get sick. He fell to his knees and allowed any remaining Gatorade in his belly to come out. Still unable to move, he fell to his side and dropped his head against the tile floor. He gazed across the linoleum as his mother continued to sob.

"You can just burn in hell with me, Steve-en!" his mother belted out with anger.

"I didn't want to do it. I had to, mom," Steven croaked from the floor. He was powerless and could do nothing but listen to the words being pushed out of his mouth. As his mother sobbed, he could faintly hear the mocking falsetto voice from the lady in the burlap sack down the hall. Looking under the bed and across the floor, he peered out into the hallway. It was pitch black.

"I couldn't take it anymore, mom. I just couldn't take all the crap from the other kids. I didn't want to, mom. I just wanted you to stop being… so crazy."

What the hell was he talking about? What did he do? What did *I* do? The realization that he was listening to the worm carrying on a conversation with his mom caused Steven to feel dizzy. His former self had been stuck in time, stuck in the right hemisphere of his brain all these years, yet it was still the same child from the time when his mother was still alive. And here it was, in complete control of his body having a heart-to-heart talk with dear old dead mom. Steven felt even more sick.

"You put me in HELL, you little bastard," his mother shouted.

"You were already in hell," Steven's child voice calmly replied. "You were in hell long before I sneaked into your hospital room and put that pillow over your head."

Steven was stunned. He couldn't believe what he was saying. Unable to move, he continued to gaze under the bed toward the dark hallway.

"I had to, mom," he whispered. "I had to."

Then it came to Steven. The memory floated up into his consciousness as he was listening to himself make the confession. He was a little boy hiding under his mother's hospital bed, lying on the tile floor in the dark. He waited forever for the nurses to make their evening rounds and for the hospital to become quiet. When he thought she had fallen asleep he climbed up on her bed and stood on his knees next to her. Looming over his mother, Steven watched her as she peacefully slept. It was a rare sight to see her in a peaceful state. She snored. He abruptly yanked a pillow out from under her head. He held it up high and then pushed it down on her face with force as he saw her awaken. Thinking back, he remembered throwing his entire upper body over the pillow in the dark hospital room. And he remembered how he had fought and fought and pleaded for her to die as she jerked against her wrist and ankle straps, screaming into the pillow. It seemed like it took an eternity before she finally collapsed into submission and had died. Steven remembered when he had finally pulled away the pillow that his mother's face was frozen in an expression of terror. Her mouth was agape, her lips stretched back. Her eyes were wide open, but the irises no longer had the hazel-green glow of life. They were gray and dull and dead. And there was young Steven, looking down without emotion upon his mother's face. He dutifully dug into his pocket and pulled out two pennies. Carefully he forced one of her eyes closed. And with his other hand he held a penny up to his face, licking it and then placing it sticky side down on top of the closed eyelid. He performed the same ritual on the other eye. Then Steven let out a small sigh as he casually wished his mother a peaceful farewell, "Bye-bye, mommy."

"I had to, mom," he again whispered.

Steven tried to force himself to move, to get up and run. He had a momentary flashback from when he had the meltdown in the cafeteria at work. It was the same paralysis but instead of just his left side being affected, his entire body was under the control of the worm, the monster.

"You didn't change a damn thing, Steven. I'm in hell. Do you hear me, Steven?" Her voice lowering a bit as she continued, "He still sneaks in my room every day and sticks me with needles. That little shit!"

She must be talking about Norman. Steven felt the ire rise inside him. Beyond the bitter taste of bile from throwing up, there were the old nails again. Steven involuntarily slammed his fist against the floor.

"Mother," Steven's child voice said sternly. "I sent that scumbag freak to hell. I chased him down and I caught him, and I sent him straight to hell."

"You sent him to my hell, God damn you, Steven! You sent him to myyyyyyyy HELLLLL!!" His mother began thrashing violently again as she cried.

Steven gazed across the tile floor trying to grasp what was being said in this bizarre dialog. He felt sick to his stomach that he, himself, had that kind of blackness within him. Whether it was today or thirty-some years ago, he had the capacity and the willingness to murder another human being. And beyond his belief, he had to accept the fact that he killed his mother out of shame and maybe to bring some sanity into his own selfish world. The word "sanity" echoed in Steven's head as he realized the irony listening to his long dead mother screaming and crying above him in the bed.

Regret filled his heart. What had he done? His life might have been completely different if he had grown up with a mom. Maybe she would have eventually gotten well enough to leave the hospital and be a normal mom, apron in the kitchen, apple pies… the whole spiel. Maybe they would have moved away, and the windmill accident might never have happened. Or then again, maybe she was destined to die in the hospital. Maybe he saved her from suffering further. No matter, it was all just too much to accept.

Drooling on the floor, Steven sank deeper into his disbelief. Could it really be he murdered his mother and then murdered Norman? A voice inside his head chimed in, "and don't forget about Uri." Then it clicked. Uri must have been behind this scheme of torture. He must have been keeping a leash of control on his mom by having that fucker Norman pump her full of heroine to keep her brain dead. He must have been doing this even as she was strapped to her bed in the mental hospital. Apparently, Norman was that fat Hungarian's evil little runner.

And now Steven could understand the source of his resentment. The empowerment he felt when he realized he had decapitated Uri. The elation knowing that he was dead. Only such satisfaction can come from holding a grudge for decades. There was definitely no regret for wasting that old man. How many others had Uri tortured? Steven considered the bag lady down the hall with her eyes pinned shut. This place was hell. And his mother would suffer in it every day, forever strapped to her bed, forced her daily syringe of poison.

Anger was building. He could sense it coming on strong. Steven bit his lower lip and immediately tasted his blood. He could feel the worm becoming frustrated and sensed the hatred turning into rage. The blood lust had returned. Everything that was happening to his mother was wrong. Everything about this place was wrong. The worm was a powder- keg and it was ready to blow. His mouth began to water. Saliva and blood dripped onto the tiles.

Again, Steven desperately tried to move but he was still paralyzed on the linoleum floor. He felt the hair rise on the back of his neck when he spotted two bare feet standing at the entrance to the room. It was Norman.

Chapter 18

The screams and cries from the crazy lady on the third floor echoed throughout the Inn. It wasn't that long ago Norman had quieted her whining by pumping her veins with the usual dosage. As much as he hated her, the routine of delivering her shots gave him purpose. It was his duty. And the agony he put her through was his reward. He believed the more times he stabbed her with the needle, the more effective he was at getting her to shut up. But most of the time he did it just for fun. Sometimes he would rapidly jab her so hard the needle would break right off of the syringe.

He found himself in the basement staring at the wall when he heard her start up again. Norman listened to her despair ringing off the pipes. While he sat on the damp floor in the corner of the utility room, he had an idea, a sinister thought. After pondering on it for a moment, he decided to go back up to the third floor.

As though the notion alone replaced the necessity to walk up all those stairs, Norman suddenly found himself floating down the third-floor hallway. He lightly touched the wall dragging his fingernail across the old wallpaper as he looked down and noticed his feet dangling about a foot above the floor. He couldn't recall ever being this delighted. The recent events at the Inn had given Norman a new outlook on his dismal existence. He couldn't put his finger on it, but it was more than just amusement. It was wonderment. But Norman also felt a newfound sense of empowerment and control. This building and all the freakish tenants were his now. They belonged to him, and he was their keeper. To Norman, the Inn was his and always will be.

Upon reaching the piercing blue light from the annoying woman's room he planted his feet down on the floor and stood in the doorway. He peered in at the woman strapped to the bed as he allowed his eyes to adjust to the offensive light. She was sobbing as usual.

Unlike the standard ritual, this time Norman wasn't holding a syringe. Instead, he held the remains of Uri's head under his arm.

"Nnnnn-nnnn-nooooooo!!" the woman shouted, apparently sensing Norman's presence.

Norman stepped into the room and held what was left of Uri's head in both hands. He no longer had a face although most of his scalp was untouched yielding an oversized white mane. All the flesh on his face had been cleanly chewed away from his skull. The jawbone was barely held in place by scant threads of sinew. Some of his teeth were missing. Any tissue that had otherwise dangled from Uri's slashed throat was gone; albeit the soft palette behind the roof of the mouth remained intact. His eyes also remained unscathed. They rotated freely in bare sockets scanning the new surroundings of the woman's room.

"Stay away from me, punk!" the scrawny lady shouted as she squirmed against her constraints.

Norman walked closer to the bed. He looked down at her coins. They looked back. Leaning over her face he found himself in a staring contest. The pennies laid on her eyes were mesmerizing.

Norman stood back and held up Uri's head by his hair. With his long floppy hand, Norman spun the head, watching as Uri's eyes darted back and forth. After a few moments when the head stopped spinning, he gently set it down on the bed atop her shoulder between the bed rail and her head. For a brief second or two the woman lay quiet and motionless. But then she felt the bony face against her cheek. And then she flipped out.

"YaaaaaaahhhhHH!!" she cried out as she violently thrashed her body upward and outward causing the bed rails to clang loudly. She threw her head from side to side and bucked hard against the mattress. The entire bed banged against the floor.

Norman watched Uri as he looked upon the flailing woman. He watched him with great anticipation but then realized that without a face there would be no expression, no reaction to encountering his former wife. And with the pennies laid on her eyes, there was no way of knowing if either of them recognized each other. None the less, Norman watched Uri with curiosity as his head bobbled about amidst the turmoil.

"Noooooooo!" the woman belted out loudly.

In a stroke of perfect timing, Uri bit hard with his fleshless mouth and managed to catch the woman's upper lip with his incisor just as she swung her face in his direction. He tightly clenched his jaw shut latching on to her flesh. She screamed even louder and continued to throw her head from side to side. Uri's head followed.

Norman rubbed his hands together. His lips stretched all of the way back to his ears exposing his tiny teeth. As he arched his eyebrows in elation, he momentarily became aware of the cuts on his forehead but chose not to touch them.

He could hear the bag lady chiming in from down the hall, "Noooo, save me, save me." As he listened to the sarcastic taunting, Norman felt himself slowly rise into the air. He was on cloud nine.

The woman on the bed stopped trying to throw the skull from her lip, conceding with one last protest. She arched her back and emitted a high-pitched howl before going completely slack. She stopped moving her head and allowed Uri's remains to rest beside her on the bed. She lay still as the faceless skull continued to glare at her from point blank range, affixed to her mouth. Norman noticed that she was contorting her fingers and toes in agony. She let out a long, cold moan.

Norman was enthralled by the morbid kiss of the newly reacquainted husband and wife. He stared at the two of them and let the image sink in. They were honeymooners, madly in love, bound in wedlock. And Norman would like nothing more than to keep them this way. They were his. They belonged to him, and this is how they should be, together, forever.

Chapter 19

Boiling with rage, Steven uncontrollably lurched underneath the bed and and took a swipe at Norman's feet with the flashlight. He missed as Norman rose above the floor. Steven sprawled out on his belly and swung again from under the bed. The flashlight made an empty swooshing sound. Grunting, he recoiled to leverage his balance and get on his knees.

Instantly, Norman was under the bed and in Steven's face. Those enormous eyes with beady black dots and his sinister grimace almost scared Steven to death. He wanted to scream, and he wanted to flee but he was powerless against the paralyzing control of the worm. Norman stretched his lips back and made a slight hissing sound. Against his will and his better judgment, Steven opened his mouth as wide as possible and roared like a lion into Norman's face. And to his surprise it was

Norman who was fleeing. He was leaving the room, rapidly moving into the hall on his tip toes.

Steven quickly lunged out from under the bed toward the door trying to get on his feet. Unfortunately, Steven wasn't a spry young boy, he was a slightly overweight, nearly middle-aged man. This miscalculation resulted in Steven slamming his shoulder against the underside of the bed rail with considerable force launching a lightning bolt of pain down his spine and into his legs. The bed vaulted upward. Steven's mother screeched out loud, "Steeee-veeen!!"

Steven got to his feet. He turned back to the bed just in time to see it topple over onto its side, spilling Uri's head onto the tile floor and burying his strapped in mother as the bed overturned on top of her. Her screams turned to muffled whimpers. Only for a moment did he consider picking up the bed before turning his focus back to Norman. He bent down to pick up the flashlight. His entire body was searing with pain as he tried with every ounce of his will to regain muscle control, but he couldn't. His right hand was no longer his reliable ally and was useless. There was just no way to penetrate the overwhelming possession over his body. And every nerve ending, from his fingers to his toes, seemed to be on fire from the internal conflict.

The flashlight's glass lens and bulb were smashed. Even though it was still a viable weapon, Steven found himself hurling it against the wall out of anger. He stomped deliberately out into the hallway. Steven felt mentally weak and was humbled. He had no free will, no choice in the matter. He was being taken for a ride in his own body and was forced to watch with his eyes wide open, tromping down the dark hallway.

"Norman! Where are you, you prick? Come out here like a man, you pussy!" Steven shouted as he pounded on the wall dislodging decades worth of dust. As he arrived at the room of the lady in the burlap sack, he kicked the door open. A cloud of dust and cobwebs wafted out into the hall. "Nooorman?" Steven whispered whimsically as he stepped into the room.

There were all the dolls, quietly roosting on the shelves. In the middle of the floor was the big brown bag. The lady with the buttons sewn on her face was squirming about from within it and crying, "Feed meeee, oh feeeeeed me."

He looked around. The room was otherwise empty. He briskly stepped over the bag and walked to the bathroom and peered in. It was too dark to see clearly but Norman wasn't there. Steven tried with difficulty to pay attention to the lady in the bag using his periphery vision, but she was behind him. He was relieved there was nothing in the bathroom and he sensed that pissed off the worm. Looking around the room, he spotted the basket full of sewing gear next to the old sewing machine. The handle of an old pair of large scissors slightly extended above the lip of the basket. He quickly moved to the basket and snatched them up.

"I'm hungry!!" shouted the lady in a disturbingly aggressive voice.

To Steven's horror, he felt the grip on the scissors tighten as he raised them to his chest. Knowing what was coming he tried to close his eyes but couldn't. Being completely paralyzed he could do nothing but watch himself backhand deliver the blades of the scissors down hard into the center of the burlap sack. He made a solid connection yet there was no reaction. The sack stood perfectly still. He retracted the weapon. Still, there was no motion and no sound. He stood up and watched carefully for any movement.

Flit, flit.... flit, flit, flit....

Pigeon wings? Steven quickly looked behind him to see what was causing the noise. There was nothing there... except a faint sprinkle of dust floating in the air.

Flit, flit, flit, flit.... flit, flit, flit....

Jerking his head back the other direction, he again saw nothing, only some dust scattering from the shelves. Steven looked closely and noticed that a few of the dolls had their eyes open. One of them had a teardrop streak of dust rolling down its cheek.

Flit, flit, flit, flit, flit, flit, flit, flit, flit, flit, flit, flit....

All the dolls' eyes were popping open. The rapid sound of the mechanical eyelids overwhelmed the room like the sound of cascading water. Dust filled the air causing Steven to squint. He pivoted on his heel and looked around the room to see each and every one of the porcelain face dolls looking at him. Even in the dimly lit room, he could see all their eyes, tiny iridescent pinpoints, one pair per doll. Steven stiffened. He sensed the worm was just as spooked as he was.

Chomp!

Steven fell to his knees in pain. He rolled to his side and retracted his legs in defense. Looking over at the bag, it was jerking back and forth, rolling towards him. The burning pain in his right calf caused him to wince and grit his teeth. Reaching down he felt the hot sensation of his blood dribble onto the palm of his hand. He lightly touched the wound through his torn slacks causing a searing pain to shoot up his leg. It was enough of a touch to confirm that a chunk of his flesh had been bitten out of his calf. Steven thought he was going to be sick again.

The bag rolled against Steven's wounded leg; he yelled in pain. With his good leg, he kicked the lady in the bag as hard as he could and sent her sliding across the floor. He noticed the chunk of his flesh fall from the bag onto the floor. Apparently, it was bitten off through the burlap material preventing it from being ingested. Steven tasted bile.

One of the dolls fell off the shelf. Its porcelain face cracked open upon hitting the floor. Steven looked into its tiny eyes; they looked back. Another doll fell to the floor a little closer to Steven. This one's face was intact and it also stared at him as it lay limp on the dirty floor. One after another, the dolls began dropping from the shelves. Some making a slight squeaking sound on impact, most cracking their delicate faces. Anticipating an avalanche of evil dolls falling on him and burying him, he quickly got to his feet. The agony of the bite wound was unbearable. It didn't matter, he had to get out. Upon attempting to boldly take a step on his bad leg, Steven shivered from the pain and fell back down on the floor onto his knees. His throat filled with airborne dust making him cough. He got on his hands and knees and tried to get back on his feet. Something sharp cut into his hand. A shard from a broken doll's face sliced a one-inch gash in his palm.

All the dolls were falling from the shelves stirring up more dust.

Steven clenched his teeth and got up on his feet knowing what to expect with the pain in his leg. He would have to just deal with it; grin and bear it. Quickly he took two steps, then allowed himself to pause for a moment but quickly resumed walking before he gave in to the pain. Each step was challenged by the debris from accumulating doll parts.

Then Steven looked around the floor and realized that they were moving. They were bending and squirming toward him, coalescing around him. This wasn't right. He had to get out now. It was almost impossible to kick the dolls out of the way without collapsing from pain. But he tried anyway. And again, Steven fell to the floor. He felt them. They weren't exactly crawling, instead they were bunching up on him as though he was drawing them like a magnet. Steven got to his knees causing two of the dolls to fall off his lap. He swung the scissors in a horizontal arc trying to clear out the pile from in front of him. Then he felt something enter his wound. The pain was excruciating. He reached down and yanked a doll from his leg and whipped it against the wall. Quickly Steven got up on his feet and was struck on the forehead by a falling doll. Almost immediately, blood dripped off Steven's brow.

Ignoring the pain in his leg, Steven took two giant steps forward. The dolls were slithering on the floor in front of him, separating him from the hallway. Steven looked back to see the burlap bag making its way to him, pushing aside the dolls as it moved along like an inchworm.

Out of desperation Steven took one big step over the pile of dolls and made a diving lunge for the door. Upon landing on more dolls, he felt cuts from the broken porcelain. Quickly Steven rolled over on his shoulder and attempted a somersault. After an awkward landing he looked up and found that he had made it to the doorway. He got to his feet and jumped out into the pitch-black hallway.

Steven looked back into the room. The dolls were no longer shapeless bundles of fabric, nylon hair and powder white faces. They were getting up on their feet and standing. They were standing up and leaning on each other for stability awkwardly trying to to make tiny steps. He didn't want to wait and see what would happen next. He slammed the door shut hard smashing a few dolls in the way. To the best of his ability, he hobbled down the hallway in the dark toward the stairs. He didn't look back.

Something bit him on the neck. He swatted at it and connected sending a doll's head to the floor where he heard its face smash into pieces. As Steven limped down the hall, he carried the scissors in his left hand while he patted about his body with his right, checking for any more of the evil little dolls hitching a ride.

The brief sense of relief from escaping the doll room abated when Steven remembered that he had zero control over what he was doing. His leg was hurting badly, and he needed to stop. But he was overruled by the worm and continued to limp toward the stairs. Upon reaching the top of the steps, Steven could make out a faint light from the lower floors. He grabbed the rail with his free hand and began to hop down each step on his good leg while holding the scissors away from his body for balance.

What was that little terror within him going to do? Again, Steven tried to fight the control over his muscles but only managed to cause more pain in his leg. He couldn't escape the notion that the tables had been turned and the roles completely reversed. For all those years he did everything he could possibly do to suppress the sinister right lobe of his brain from lashing out at him. But he lost the battle and now he was the one being suppressed. In trying to resist his movement, the stress on his muscles caused his back to ache and his head to pound.

Steven figured he would give the worm a taste of his own medicine and decided he would imagine loud annoying bagpipe music. He concentrated on a single droning tone. Then he raised the horrible screeching sound of the multiple reeds in his head making it as loud as he could possibly imagine.

He stopped hopping down the steps when he reached the landing halfway down to the second floor. In a not-so-subtle gesture to get Steven to stop the music, the blades of the scissors were pointed to his right eye about an inch away. So, he decided to stop the crappy bagpipe music.

He pulled the scissors aside and continued to hop down toward the second floor. Reaching out to grab the handrail, Steven ran directly into Uri, as the armless, headless Hungarian was blindly walking up the stairs.

Steven tried to catch his breath as he felt the force of gravity carry his weight onto Uri's fat belly as both toppled down the stairs. Steven fell hard on his back against the wooden steps knowing that Uri could land on him like a cement truck and crush him. Instead, Uri bounced over Steven just grazing his chest. But he was unable to move his hand out of the way in time as Uri planted his hip against Steven's arm instantly smashing the bones in his wrist and hand, causing him to release the scissors. Uri rapidly rolled down the stairs. Steven followed, hitting his face, his knee and his shoulder against the hard steps before reaching the second floor.

Dazed, Steven groaned as he tried to get up. His vision was blurred, he was dizzy. He noticed Uri trying to push himself against the wall attempting to get his little feet under his mammoth belly. He noticed the broken wooden handle from the shovel still protruding from Uri's neck.

His arm began throbbing. He held it limply to his chest and noticed his hand looked slightly twisted as it began to swell. His pinkie finger spasmed. Looking back up the stairs he spotted the metallic glint of the scissors. The pain in his leg was excruciating, nonetheless, he hobbled up a few steps and grabbed the scissors with his good hand.

Limping over to Uri, Steven held the scissors above his head. Again, he wanted to close his eyes, knowing what he was about to do. But before the worm could bury the blades into Uri's chest, Steven heard laughter coming from down the hall. It was raspy and decrepit like a cackling witch. Steven squinted to try and make out whatever it was at the end of the hallway. All he could see was the silhouette of a short figure with frizzy hair, holding up something shiny. He could tell it was a woman wearing an apron as she stood in the partial light from an opened door.

Suddenly he was knocked to the ground, bumped from behind by Uri's round belly. Quickly Steven rolled to his side avoiding Uri's crushing mass as the Hungarian made a loud thud falling on the floor. Even without a head, Uri was smart enough to know that his mountain of a torso was a formidable weapon.

Steven got on his feet holding the scissors and his damaged left hand against his chest. He looked down the hall and saw that the woman in the apron was slowly advancing. She wasn't walking or running. Instead, she seemed to be gliding. Actually, she was dragging her feet as she floated forward. Steven could hear the scraping of her shoes on the floor.

Once the wiry-haired old woman came within twenty feet, it became apparent her head was cocked back with her mouth gaping wide open. And the witch was wearing black sunglasses. She was crooked forward, knees bent with her thin arms spread outward, holding a large meat cleaver. As she came closer, Steven looked in horror as he realized that she didn't have any feet. Below her knees there was only a bit of flesh partially covering her shin bones. The protruding white bones from each leg tapered off to a point as though they had been whittled. Steven shivered when he realized that it was the grotesque brittle bones that were screeching against the floor.

Chills went up Steven's spine when the old woman gagged on her laughter. He tried to move but couldn't. He was still in the grip of the worm, who was also frozen in terror.

"Move, damn it!" Steven desperately urged himself.

The witch was closing in, the scraping on the floor getting louder.

Steven stopped breathing when he saw the shiny edge of the cleaver raised above her head. She was close enough that he could see her pale skin, it was so thin it was transparent. He could see her skull through her face. His heart pounded with force. It was all he could do to finally break the paralysis and step backwards. The crazy looking old hag picked up speed. Steven felt the pain in his leg as he took a few more steps back toward the stairs. The old woman rushed in on him whipping the cleaver around in a twirling motion above her head.

Uri suddenly plodded aimlessly in front of Steven. The old witch paused for a moment glaring at Uri. And then with the speed of light, the cleaver flew from the hag's hand, streaking through the air and landing directly in the center of Uri's gut, completely burying its handle and all. She cackled loudly, echoing up and down the hallway.

Steven turned to the stairs and tried to run. He gingerly hobbled on his leg ignoring the pain as he gasped in fear. He held the scissors and his broken hand against his chest. The stairs were slick with dust. He would have to do his best to avoid slipping without being able to hold the rail. Sweat and blood stung his eyes, his mouth was dry and tasted acidic. Steven reminded himself to breathe.

After getting past the first two steps, he was confident he wasn't going to slip and fall. He heard the witch cackling above him but chose not to look back. Not only was he afraid to see that she might be swooping down on him, but he knew he was doomed to fall on his face if he didn't stay focused on the steps ahead. With only a few steps remaining, he jumped to the landing putting most of his weight on his good leg. Taking small steps, Steven rounded the corner and started down the final flight of steps. He knew the pain was there, but he was also aware of the surging adrenaline in his veins.

Seeing the yellow-brown glow of the lights in the parlor, Steven sensed how close he was to the front of the building. The feeling of being out of the Inn and into his Land Rover was enticing. It was within reach. He just needed to be deliberate and swift and make a run for it. He considered Uri's corpse blocking the front door, the rotting corpse from the so-called real world. He would still have to get around it. Steven considered the window instead. He could toss one of the end tables through it. Getting cut by glass seemed inconsequential at this point. He knew what had to be done, he was close to being free and his spirits were up. It didn't hurt to accompany the adrenaline with an emotional lift.

Norman was standing at the bottom of the stairs.

Steven stopped in his tracks.

Norman slowly looked up from his feet following the steps until he looked directly up at Steven. He stretched his lips back and gave an evil grin.

Steven growled uncontrollably. He hopped down two more steps and jumped over the rest to the first floor. Landing awkwardly the pain was unbearable. Staying on his feet, he looked out into the parlor. Then he saw Norman running down the steps into the basement. Steven quickly hobbled after him gritting his teeth, tightly clenching the scissors.

To his dismay, he wasn't leaving the Inn.

When Steven reached the cold cement floor of the basement, he peered down the narrow, dimly lit hall. There was the familiar dirty glow emanating from the utility room about halfway down. There was no sign of Norman. But Steven knew. He knew Norman was hiding under the pipes. It was his place to run away, and Steven had him cornered.

Panting heavily, Steven limped down the hall. He held his broken hand to his chest while holding the pair of scissors up at shoulder height. He knew what he had to do. He had to send that little bastard Norman to hell. Send that turd straight to hell!

Steven stopped at the door and looked inside the room. How many hours have passed since he had found himself here, lying on the floor in the dark?

"Normy…?" Steven's child voice said coyly. "Come out and play, Normy."

Steven stepped into the room and looked around. It was empty. Crouching down he looked under the pipes but there was nothing there. He stood quietly and listened to the water dripping on the floor. He looked at the pipes, how shiny they were. He could see his own reflection repeated in the menagerie.

The door of the clothes dryer flung open. Norman's head popped out. Like a monkey he deftly pulled his little body out of the dryer and stood atop it. He stared for a moment but then looked up towards the ceiling. Bending down and gathering his might, Norman leaped upward extending his arms high forcing open the clothes chute trap door. He had managed to push the door open and was climbing up and out, escaping. But Steven lunged forward, dropping the scissors on the floor as he reached out and grabbed Norman's ankle. Yanking him down, Norman got his left hand caught in the chute door as it was jerked closed. He was dangling in midair, hanging helplessly with his feet kicking just a few inches above the washer and dryer.

Steven picked up the scissors and held them high. He turned to Norman and scowled at him. Then he said, "You don't get to die in peace, you little prick." and plunged the scissors into Norman's chest, into an existing wound.

Steven tried but couldn't look away. He was powerless and could only watch the scene unfold from the vantage point of his own eyes. It was the same scene from over thirty years ago, chasing Norman down and cornering him in the utility room, watching his face drain with defeat upon getting caught in the clothes chute door. And then torturing and killing him. Besides remembering how it all had unraveled years ago, Steven had recaptured exactly how it felt, the thrill of vengeance and sense of empowerment. He also remembered that he had a bicycle waiting outside for him back then.

Looking at Norman's face, Steven looked over the cuts he had given him all those years ago. It was like leaving a signature on a piece of art. He stepped back and admired his work while at the same time he felt sick to his stomach; he was a savage killer. Without expression, Norman touched the cuts on his face with his free hand. Steven pulled the scissors out of Norman's chest. All the while Norman hung passively from the chute door just staring at Steven as they went through the familiar motions.

This impromptu reenactment brought Steven full circle back to the basement where years ago the murder of Norman unfolded. And it was a big day back then for Steven, killing his mom and then chasing down

Norman and slashing away at him. The truth was always there, buried in Steven's history for decades. And now he stood dumbfounded watching the rerun of those events. The shiny pipes reflected Norman's wide-eyed, blank stare. Steven took a few steps back holding the scissors to his side and stood motionless as he gathered in the realization of the moment. Still slightly out of breath, he closed his eyes and listened to the random water droplets echoing off the cinder block walls. He felt woozy. He was overwhelmed with a hundred different emotions and thought he might faint.

Like a spider racing up a strand of web, chills climbed up Steven's spine when he suddenly felt a set of cold, sharp fingernails lightly caress the skin on the back of his neck. His scalp crawled setting off a shiver down his back to his knees. Looking up, he noticed more than just Norman's eyes reflecting in the pipes, he also saw a pair of black sunglasses.

Instinctively Steven spun to his knee and held up his forearm in defense. He squinted looking past the scissors he held in his raised hand. The old woman chortled and guffawed and then she gagged and coughed. She leaned her body forward and in a split second she ripped the scissors out of Steven's hand like taking candy away from a baby. With her face pointed upward away from Steven, she held the scissors up to her nose and gave them a sniff. Steven heard the whiff of the scissors ripping through the air before he realized the witch had torn a gash across his chest from his left shoulder down to his lower right ribs. She let out a roar of laughter through her gaping wide mouth. This didn't happen thirty years ago.

Steven fell back on his butt. He didn't have to touch his chest to know there was warm blood seeping to the surface of his skin.

Norman was grinning ear to ear. The crotchety old woman with the wiry hair arched her back and stood upward grotesquely causing her mouth to open even wider. Steven thought she might swoop down and swallow him like a snake. Instead, she glided a few feet on her tapered shin bones toward Norman, leaving scratch marks on the cement floor.

Almost surprising himself, Steven was on his feet and lunging behind the witch toward the door. He was fully aware of the searing pain in his calf but that didn't stop him from putting every ounce of strength into it. Once he hit the hallway floor, he leaned forward raising his knees high pounding his feet down like pistons. He held his smashed and swollen left hand against his bloody chest, briefly realizing his sweater was tattered. He was moving fast. As he reached the stairs at the end of the hall, he looked back and gasped when he saw the silhouette of the witch standing outside of the utility room. Steven scrambled up the stairs. Panting, he rounded the landing and headed up to the parlor. Every muscle in his body was burning. He felt weak but kept pumping his legs. As he reached the first floor, his lungs ached as he gasped for air. He was running on fumes. If it wasn't for the shear adrenaline running through his veins, he would have collapsed.

Steven felt a small sense of relief when he looked across the long parlor to see the curtains pulled back from a window near the front of the room exposing the outside world. It was still night.

Without looking back to the stairs, Steven rushed between the rows of sofas and end tables. He tried to mostly hop on his good leg until it started tightening up with a cramp. His breath was labored making a harsh wheezing sound as he fought to inhale. He used his good hand to pull himself forward along the furniture. He was within twenty feet of the window.

He looked for something he could grab and launch through the glass. He considered a lamp, but it would likely only crack the windowpane. Steven knew he would have to give it everything he had into picking up one of these end tables and heaving it. He spotted his choice. Without breaking step, Steven reached down and grabbed the leg of a small, two-foot-wide table. Keeping his bad arm against his chest, he raised the table off the floor tossing a lamp as he swung it forward. Steven stopped five feet short of the window and pivoted on his left foot spinning the table around him in a 360-degree arc. He let the table go in a one-handed hammer throw and felt an immediate sense of elation when it crashed through the window. "Don't look back, don't look back, don't look...." Steven muttered to himself.

He paused before attempting to leap through the window. There were large shards protruding from the windowsill that could easily kill him if he should land on one. He swiped his foot along the edge knocking out a few of the larger pieces. He moved his body sideways to throw his butt out first and hopefully would land outside on his back.

Looking back down the parlor, he saw the old witch rushing at him. She was floating in the air with her head cocked back and the scissors raised high. Steven panicked. He turned and tried to dive out of the window, but it was too late. The old witch dug her sharp claw into Steven's shoulder from behind and whipped him around as she let out a loud raspy cackle. As Steven raised both his hands to his face for protection, he saw a tiny glint of light reflect off the blades of the scissors as she sent them flying directly toward his eye. He tried to dodge his head to the left, but the scissors connected with his forehead just above his right brow, the blades burying deep into his brain.

Steven instinctively grabbed the handles of the scissors. They were planted firmly in his skull. Losing his balance, he sat back against the windowsill unaware of the broken glass cutting into him. He looked at the old witch. She was reaching out toward him with her long bony fingers and long, cracked nails. She was reaching out to his chest, his heart.

Steven's vision was beginning to fade. The brownish-yellow parlor light emanating from the dirty low ceiling was turning gray. The image of the horrible old woman in sunglasses was also beginning to fade. He gasped and closed his eyes when he felt the disturbing sensation of her hand entering his chest and cupping his heart in an ice-cold clutch. His whole body froze, his spine stiffening. And then he felt his beating heart come to an abrupt stop. Steven knew he was going to die.

Fading from consciousness, he felt the world spinning, turning from gray to black, spiraling down a bottomless pit. His life was rapidly quieting into a dull silence... Nothing but numbness. Nothing but darkness.

Steven sensed peace. He was calm and felt like he was floating. And he could sense his face. It was cool and tingly. Then to his surprise he became aware of his shallow breathing. He licked his lips. They were wet. Slowly Steven began to come around hearing rain drops on the crisp leaves near his head. He tried to open his eyes, the moisture on his eyelashes causing him to blink. He turned his head to his side. He was lying in the mud. He slowly reached up and touched the scissor handles sticking out of his forehead. The slight nudge sent an odd twitch in his brain causing him to see a flash of silver light. The entire left side of his face spasmed in unison.

The cool wet sensation of the mud seeped through his clothes. He became aware of the pain in his leg and the heat emanating from the gash on his chest. He thought about his crushed hand but couldn't feel it. It had gone numb. Blinking away the raindrops, he considered the time of day. It was still dark. Putting some weight on his good hand, Steven attempted to sit up. But he simply could not lift his head. Instead, he rolled onto his left shoulder dragging his head in the mud. Once he was on his knees, he again tried to lift his head. This was only possible for a moment as he allowed the left side of his face to fall back in the mud carefully keeping the scissor handles from touching the ground.

But once he was able to look up, Steven opened his eyes and caught a glimpse of his Land Rover parked about twenty feet away. It seemed like a mile. Again, he tried to lift his head. Now he felt the throbbing pain begin to rise as his vision blurred. He felt nauseous.

Before his aching head fell back to the mud, he caught it and held it up using the forearm of his crushed wrist and hand. He looked around. His vision had narrowed to a tunnel, the margin of his periphery had completely blurred. Looking at his vehicle he felt a yearning for its security. He had to try and stand up. With his weight on his right knee, he picked up his left foot and put it on the ground. Shifting his weight on it, he then tried to get up on both feet. Feeling dizzy and nauseous, the feeble attempt was quickly aborted, and Steven went back on his knees. Still holding his head up with his left arm, he looked down to the mud. He knew he was going to have to crawl the distance to his car.

Steven imagined himself as a dilapidated old horse as he took to relocating his hand in the muck and then slowly forcing his knees to follow suit. He pointed himself to his left toward the Land Rover. His ears were ringing. His leg throbbed. Steven focused on his balance and keeping his eyes open. After a few minutes he raised his head high enough to look up and see he was about halfway there. He closed his eyes and plodded forward. After a few more moments he looked up and was disappointed he had only advanced just a few more feet. He had to be patient. He was going to get there as long as he didn't overdo it and cause himself to pass out.

It didn't take much longer before Steven felt his shoulder touch one of the tires. He was on the passenger side of the car. Instead of going around to the driver's side, he moved down along the car until he was able to reach up and grab the passenger door handle. It was locked. In a flash of panic, Steven wondered if he even had the keys with him. With his upper body leaning against the door, he reached down into his pocket and was overwhelmed with relief when he felt the metallic keys in his pocket. Without taking them out, he touched the automatic door unlock button on the control attached to his key ring. The Land Rover responded with a flash of parking lights, two beeps and the click of the doors unlocking. Steven reached back to the door handle and opened it. He had to lean back to avoid the door as it arced outward. Steven reached up and felt the dry soft wool from the seat cover. He grasped at the fabric as he pushed up on his feet continuing to hold his head up with his bad arm. It took a few minutes, but Steven managed to work his way up into the vehicle and crawl into the driver's seat.

Sitting behind the wheel, he reached back into his pocket and pulled out the keys. He held his breath as he put the largest key into the ignition. What a relief when the car started almost immediately. Still cradling his head, Steven had to reach across the steering wheel to flip on the headlights. Then he managed to feel his way to the switch to turn on the wipers. He had to get going, get to a hospital or somewhere for help before losing consciousness. Steven took a moment to get his bearings and figure out the direction of the road. It was behind him to his left.

Without hesitation, Steven stuck the transmission into first gear and stepped on the gas. He rocked to his right as the car turned to the left as the tires tentatively took hold in the muddy driveway. He could barely see ahead into the dark but managed to drive out onto the road. He took a right but had no sense of where he was going. Steven's scope of vision was dwindling down to just a point. He didn't have long. He needed to find a Seven-Eleven or a gas station but couldn't see beyond the headlights barely able to make out the streetlights as they passed overhead. Steven started to panic and sped up. He concentrated intently on driving straight and staying on the road but was aware he was swerving in and out of his lane.

It was increasingly harder to keep his eyes open. He knew he was starting to fade. He had to quickly find some place to stop. Putting more pressure on the accelerator, Steven sped up to fifty miles per hour. Continuing to prop his head up, he instinctively moved it slightly and glanced to his right. Norman was sitting in the passenger seat with his toothy grin and wide eyes, staring at Steven. Steven freaked and reacted by jerking the steering wheel causing the Land Rover to veer to the left and jump over a curb. Trying to regain control, he overcompensated to the right and sent the speeding car rolling. Steven was sent flying out of the passenger side window. With a thud he landed hard against the pavement and tumbled awkwardly with his arms flailing before settling on his back. The Land Rover rolled a total of three times before dismantling a mail repository and coming to rest against a parked car.

With both his eyes wide open, Steven looked up into the rain and quietly watched as the streetlight above slowly dimmed to darkness.

Chapter 20

The annoying, loud footsteps of those giant hooves clomping down the long, tiled hall echoed from one end of the floor to the other. Nurse Pig had started her shift. Why the six feet, two-hundred-pound woman would want to wear waffle-stomping boots while she worked was beyond Steven. Maybe they were intended to increase her intimidation factor.

The long wait sitting in the physical therapy room was the worst of the day. But thankfully it was the last wait of the grueling Wednesday schedule. The morning began at 5:00am with the usual blood samples and vitals. This was followed by a brief visit from the speech therapist to check and see if Steven miraculously found his voice overnight. A crummy breakfast was then served in the blue dining room at 7:00am leading to the first wait of the day. It would usually take until a few minutes after 8 o'clock by the time a nurse got around to push him in his wheelchair back to his room.

By 8:45am, Monday through Friday, Steven was wheeled to the mental therapy room where he was parked alongside other despondent patients in a semicircle around a bug-faced teenager who volunteered two weeks out of the month to hold up pictures of fruits and vegetables and trees while a nurse observed reactions. Steven was good at not reacting because, in fact, he didn't give a shit about those stupid pictures. Every week it was the same thing. Why couldn't they throw caution to the wind and maybe show pictures of trains or airplanes for Christ's sake. Maybe that was too much for the other patients who occasionally let out a groan or a fart if they liked the picture being held up.

Two hours of that nonsense was enough to make anyone at this mental institute go crazy. But by 11:30am, thankfully it was back to his room where Steven watched TV or stared at the wall for an hour until it was time to wheel off to the blue dining room for lunch. Nurse Pig occasionally was on shift during lunch and made Steven sit at the drool table where the patients had to be hand fed. Even though Steven was fully capable of feeding himself, brushing his teeth, shaving and wiping his butt, he found that his lack of popularity among the staff often resulted in undesirable mealtime seating arrangements. No matter. Steven simply continued to purport a complete void of interest or bother.

After an hour in the blue dining room, before lunch completely settled, Steven was sent down to the first floor to the physical therapy wing where there were four large rooms filled with various equipment including a wading pool and sauna. Steven never got to use the sauna. Instead, he was relegated to the cold room with the free-weights and parallel bars. Two or more orderlies were required to help him get on and off the exercise equipment and to encourage him by barking at him. It was usually after 3:30pm before Steven was done with his therapy sessions and was ready to go back to his room for a quick nap before dinner.

But then he must wait. Sitting in his wheelchair, he must wait and wait until the next shift of nurses hit the floor and someone figures out there is a patient somewhere who is growing cobwebs waiting to be moved. It was always after 4:00pm by the time a nurse would show up, ruining any plans for a decent snooze.

Nurse Pig must have taken over five hundred tiny steps with her loud hooves before arriving at the physical therapy weight room. Steven looked up at her through his furrowed brow but said nothing. The nurse said nothing in return and proceeded to push Steven down the hall to the elevator. As the doors closed shut behind them, the hectic atmosphere from the first floor of the mental hospital yielded to the silence of the swift elevator, except for the nurse's obtuse nose whistle.

Steven had been at this facility for the past six weeks. Before that he had spent two months at the downtown hospital where he had first been rushed to the ER after police found him lying unconscious in the street. Although he remembers very little of it, Steven was in critical condition in the ICU for two weeks following the seven hours of surgery to remove the pair of scissors from his brain and to resolve a slight bit of internal bleeding. He then spent the toughest three weeks of his recovery isolated in his hospital bed being fed through tubes and urinating through a catheter. Steven was moved from the hospital to the mental facility once it was determined he was beyond infection and the physical healing process was well under way. Other than a few strange side effects to his ocular depth perception, his only real physical problem was his lack of coordination. Apparently, he had damaged a part of the brain that manages the movement of his legs and his ability to sit straight up. But to Steven's amazement, the progress he had made in retraining his brain was rapid and substantial. Maybe he would always have an awkward limp or maybe a tilt to his walk but there was no doubt in his mind that he would soon be on his feet and finally get rid of the wheelchair and his dependency on others to get around.

He was unable to move himself around in his wheelchair because his left hand was in a cast hanging in a sling around his neck. He required nine metal pins inserted into his wrist and hand to stabilize the countless bone fractures and ligament damage. So, for now he would just have to put up with the nurses' condescending authority and wait for them to push him back and forth.

As the elevator doors opened and Steven was being pushed down the sterile hall back to his room, he thought about how long he would allow himself to stay at this facility. He knew he probably had at least another three weeks of physical therapy before he could adequately walk on his own, but certainly they would not release him until he demonstrated a miraculous recovery of his speech, and in general, an appreciable recovery of his brain power.

His plan from the beginning, the plan he had conjured up soon after being moved out of the ICU, was to remain completely silent and act as though he was mentally stunted. Even in the dire condition following the first stages of his recovery, Steven had the sense to know that he needed time. He needed time to think through all the events that took place at the Inn and understand where he stood in his lifelong battle for sanity. And he needed time to avoid any questioning from the law in case someone happened to stumble onto the Inn and come across the decapitated corpse of old Uri. Steven knew his blood and fingerprints were all over that horrible building. But he also knew that it could be years before someone wondered upon that property and found the carnage. So far, the police had only wanted to know how he crashed his car and why he just so happened to be holding a pair of scissors during the accident. The police didn't have the patience for a brain-dead moron so there was no further questioning.

The long hallway back to Steven's room smelled of alcohol and death. He didn't know how but he would have to learn to tolerate it. The crazies on this floor were usually quiet, subdued on lithium. The violent ones were on the second floor in the fenced in rooms. Some of them had to be constantly restrained. Traipsing down the hallway was Steven's favorite character. The guy did a perfect take off the Monty Python silly walk routine. It was like he was constantly doing a water ballet on his feet. Where in the world was his mind? What was it really like to be insane? If he was faking it, he was brilliant.

Was it irony or coincidence that landed Steven in the same mental institute where his mother had spent the last days of her life? He sighed with the thought that this is where she died, where he had suffocated her all those years ago. Steven forced himself to quickly dismiss the image of his dead mother with the pennies stuck to her eyes, lying in her hospital bed with clumps of needles in her arms and legs and neck.

As the wheelchair wheels squeaked in unison, Steven and the nurse passed an open door to one of the recreation and game rooms. Steven was blinded when he glanced in and the bright light from an outside window spilled over him. In a surprising spontaneous reaction, Steven quickly caught the attention of the nurse by grunting and waving his good hand pointing back to the room they had just passed. Nurse Pig obliged and turned the wheelchair around and took him into the brightly lit room where there were only three patients sitting around, dawdling and drooling. The TV was turned off and the room was restfully quiet. Even as Steven was being wheeled into the room he continued to grunt and groan and kick his feet as he pointed at the window across the room. He settled down when he felt a mild backhanded whack to the back of his head from his favorite nurse.

Steven squinted as he was led to the window. The nurse parked the wheelchair and left the room. Steven acclimated to the light and peered out into the world. Whiteness. Pure white snow covered the landscape. There was no sign of the roads or houses or trees or bushes or hills or parks. Only softly rounded shapes could be detected under the thick blanket of pure, white, crystal, puffy snow. It was beautiful.

After a few minutes of looking out into the blissfulness of winter, Steven closed his eyes. How long has it been? Did he really waste the better part of his life straining and fighting every day just to maintain a minimal appearance of being normal? Was he so consumed by the balance of his sanity that he never ever stopped once to appreciate the millions upon billions of unique ice flakes that accumulate from the sky during a winter storm?

The first waking moments following Steven's long surgery was the realization that he was indeed safe in a hospital. His next realization was that he was free. It was obvious and it was ... unnatural. It was like an enormous weight off his chest, he felt tons lighter. He knew the evil child that was born from his past and dwelt in the right hemisphere of his brain was finally gone. He didn't have to ignore it or pacify it or hide from it any longer. Steven thought about how the left side of his body felt. Other than his hand being somewhat itchy in its cast, it felt the way it was supposed to feel. It felt like it belonged to him.

He figured he could probably stay in this facility for another four months, five tops. After that he would most certainly lose his mind and might even build a dependency on the care he has been receiving. He was told that his work benefits had run out and he was at the mental hospital courtesy of the state taxpayers. Apparently, the world was a safer place because of it.

By the time he eventually started walking, he figured he could introduce a few flashes of brilliance like saying the word "broccoli" or drawing a stick figure. And then he could slowly come out with short sentences and then eventually convey ideas and speak in complete thoughts. That should provide plenty of time to really think this out and decide on the next steps, where to live, what to do for a living. Success in his new life could be ensured with a bit of patience and careful planning. And it would be easy to turn over a new leaf, it was just a matter of playing the amnesia game and selectively remembering only the necessary parts of his past life. The world was his to define from scratch. No reason to hastily jump out into it blindly.

Steven's grandmother came to mind, and he thought about her in a whole new light. What that woman must have gone through. Her daughter was a complete whacked out junkie and her grandson was a ruthless killer. Did she know it was Steven who killed her only daughter? Only Grandma could have known how much of an evil little bastard Steven was before the windmill accident. And of course, she knew very well the shade of evil he possessed after the accident. But how much did she really know about him? What about the Inn? She surely must have known Uri but what about Norman? Did Grandma know that crazy witch with the sunglasses?

A wave of nausea hit Steven when he considered the possibility that his grandmother knew about other terrible things he might have done when he was an evil little boy. What if he had killed others? Were there other vengeful ghosts out there just like Norman? Steven thought about his mother. And again, he quickly dismissed the thought of her rotting corpse.

Looking over the bright white landscape from the window of the mental hospital, Steven looked out across the valley to the house-dotted hills at the edge of town. He could faintly see smoke emitting from some of the chimneys although the houses were invisible under the snow. Staring out in the distance he noticed a tiny shard of black, so small it looked like a missing puzzle piece in the white vista. It was a corner of the Inn peeking over the treetops.

Steven was aware that his heart rate picked up a little. He took a deep breath and relaxed in his wheelchair. He didn't need to look back to verify whether it was real or not. During the long hours of spacing-out in the mental therapy sessions, Steven was able to repeatedly go over every instant he experienced from that night at the Inn. It wasn't just a nightmare. He knew better than to give himself credit for dreaming up such a scenario that resulted in a bite of flesh from his leg, a crushed hand, cuts all over his body and a pair of scissors lodged in his forehead. It was too fantastic to *not* be real.

A patient sitting nearby choked on something. Nurse Pig quickly ran back into the room and bent him forward squeezing his chest from behind. Thankfully he spit up whatever was caught in his throat before the nurse resorted to using her big boot on the patient's backside. The silly-walk guy sauntered down the hallway glancing into the room at the brief commotion. Maybe he thought he was Fred Astaire or Gene Kelly. Always entertaining.

The notion of an existence after death gnawed at Steven. He was briefly privileged, or cursed, with the ability to have one leg in each world at the same time. It will probably always boggle his mind when he thinks of the bloody, headless corpse of Uri blocking the door while at the same time a ghostly, yet equally fat Uri roamed the halls looking for his head. All of those ghouls at the condemned Inn had past lives and now they go on in a different sense, stuck in an endless rut, mired by their evil ways. It occurred to Steven that he's already had two past lives and is now embarking on his third.

Steven remembered when he was a teenager and trying to survive the worst time of his life. His grandmother would always say something to him that never meant very much until now, "... You've only lived but a sliver of your life."

Chapter 21

Norman sat near the corner of his room, staring. He listened to the sound of grinding coming from down the hall as he touched the cuts on his face with his long, floppy hand. The room was dark all but for a wedge of light splaying on the ceiling through the cracked door.

He could hear heavy footsteps slowly plodding about in the parlor. Uri was usually wondering around down there. Sometimes he made his way up the stairs and once he even came so far down the hallway as Norman's room. It was no surprise he would go no further in the direction towards Mrs. Crawford's room. He had foolishly visited her room one last time since she had chopped off his arms leaving him with short, fatty stubs. The moment Mrs. Crawford sensed he was in her room, presumably still looking for his head, she decided he needed a special manicure, similar to the one he had given her way back when. As a result, Uri's stubby arms were tapered to a point, the flesh twisted and torn, wrapped around small protruding shards of his humerus bones. The pointed stubs of his arms almost matched the broken shovel handle still sticking out of his neck. As Uri had once discovered, the meat grinder was the perfect tool for this sort of cosmetic surgery. He was lucky to still have his feet.

Norman's vision diminished as he once again began to fade into the shadows of his room. Just as he drifted off into his usual void, he thought he heard something metallic, like loose keys falling on the floor somewhere in the building. He thought maybe the sound was coming from the basement. Was someone tapping on the pipes?

Regaining his awareness, he found himself sitting in the corner of the utility room in the basement leaning against the old boiler. He was staring at the pipes. They stared back with the reflection of his wide opened blank eyes. He listened. The floor above creaked from Uri walking around. Norman could faintly hear the undercurrent of the metallic sound, almost like chimes. He could tell it was coming from the third floor.

After a few moments of listening to the clinking sounds in the building emanating from the pipes, he rose to his feet and walked over to the clothes dryer. He opened the lid just a crack and peered in. Uri's head was safely stowed away, hidden from his brainless body. Uri darted his eyes back and forth from within his deep eye sockets before Norman let the lid fall closed.

For whatever reason, Uri never walked down into the basement. Norman was assured of solitude in his favorite place in the Inn, under the pipes in the utility room.

It occurred to Norman that the crazy bitch up on the third floor hadn't been up to her usual level of moping and crying. Normally it was almost constant. He stood for a moment and looked up at the ceiling as he crooked his head, so his ear was facing the pipes. He listened. Was she trying to trick him into thinking she didn't need her shot? Did she think she could get away with missing her routine dose? Norman was angry.

In the instant Norman decided it was time for the needle, he found himself floating down the long dark hallway of the third floor. He was prepared with three syringes in his right hand. The harsh blue light from the scrawny woman's room could be seen down the hall. As he passed the bag lady's room, he heard a soft groan. She was always hungry.

Again, the tinny sound of keys could be heard. They were coming from down the hall, from the crazy woman's room. Norman stopped and stood on his toes and listened. It was music. He realized the sound he had been hearing was coming from the light hammering of strings on a piano. The slow melody echoed down the hall. Norman cautiously walked toward the music.

As he approached the opened door to the woman's room, he paused for a moment to allow his eyes to acclimate to the offensive light. The music was distorted. Even though it was obviously coming from within the room it had a distant quality as though it was being played loudly through a telephone.

Norman stood at the doorway peering into the room. As his eyes recovered from the glare, he looked over to the right at her bed. But she wasn't there. The straps on the bed rails had been unbuckled. Beyond the bed Norman saw the cornucopia-shaped bell of a phonograph sitting on the floor. The scratchy music began to wane. But before the song could finish, Norman was startled by a loud screech. The heavy arm of the phonograph was recklessly reset to the beginning of the song. Norman could see the straggled hair of the skinny woman's head next to the phonograph. Apparently, she had been lying on the floor. As the piano ballad started up again the woman rose to her feet. To keep her balance, she awkwardly extended her long bony arms away from her sides. Once she stood erect, she pivoted on her left foot slowly turning her body as she raised her right knee into the air. Then she semi-gracefully touched the top of her head with the tips of her fingers in a ballerina's death pose.

She awkwardly moved along with the music. Her skeletal body barely held up the hospital gown. She took four tiny steps on her toes, stopped and pivoted and took two more clumsy steps before stopping for a moment. She repeated this pattern as she moved her hands in an expressive motion although her contorted fingers and bruised arms conveyed a morbid theme.

It seemed with every movement the frail body of the decrepit woman was on the threshold of collapsing to the floor. Norman was entranced by the dull pennies that remained stuck to her eyelids. It was almost as though she was looking off into the distance enraptured in a gaze.

As the macabre dance continued, Norman looked to the left of the bed and to his astonishment there was a boy sitting Indian style on the floor watching the woman stiffly move to the piano music. He looked down at the boy and saw that he had an unusually large gash on his head that extended from his forehead all the way to the back of his skull. It was so big and wide that Norman could look deep down into the center of the boy's split brain.

The boy apparently became aware of Norman's presence. While continuing to maintain his legs in a crossed position, the boy began to rise up off of the floor. As he floated upward, he slowly turned until he was looking face to face, eye to eye at Norman. In his right hand the boy held up a large pair of scissors and pointed them at Norman. He then held out his clenched left hand, rotating it until it faced upward. Slowly opening his fingers, Norman could see he was holding something. It looked to be a pair of dead insects, maybe caterpillars or centipedes.

The instant Norman recognized his own eyelids, the door violently slammed shut in his face.

* 9 7 9 8 8 8 7 0 3 3 3 3 4 *